THE PELICAN SHAKESPEARE

GENERAL EDITOR ALFRED HARBAGE

ANTONY AND CLEOPATRA

WILLIAM SHAKESPEARE

ANTONY AND CLEOPATRA

EDITED BY MAYNARD MACK

PENGUIN BOOKS

Penguin Books
625 Madison Avenue
New York, New York 10022

First published in *The Pelican Shakespeare* 1960
This revised edition first published 1970
Reprinted 1971, 1974, 1976, 1977

Printed in the United States of America by
Kingsport Press, Inc., Kingsport, Tennessee
Set in Monotype Ehrhardt

CONTENTS

PUBLISHER'S NOTE

Soon after the thirty-eight volumes forming *The Pelican Shakespeare* had been published, they were brought together in *The Complete Pelican Shakespeare*. The editorial revisions and new textual features are explained in detail in the General Editor's Preface to the one-volume edition. They have all been incorporated in the present volume. The following should be mentioned in particular:

The lines are not numbered in arbitrary units. Instead all lines are numbered which contain a word, phrase, or allusion explained in the glossarial notes. In the occasional instances where there is a long stretch of unannotated text, certain lines are numbered in italics to serve the conventional reference purpose.

The intrusive and often inaccurate place-headings inserted by early editors are omitted (as is becoming standard practise), but for the convenience of those who miss them, an indication of locale now appears as first item in the annotation of each scene.

In the interest of both elegance and utility, each speech-prefix is set in a separate line when the speaker's lines are in verse, except when these words form the second half of a pentameter line. Thus the verse form of the speech is kept visually intact, and turned-over lines are avoided. What is printed as verse and what is printed as prose has, in general, the authority of the original texts. Departures from the original texts in this regard have only the authority of editorial tradition and the judgment of the Pelican editors; and, in a few instances, are admittedly arbitrary.

SHAKESPEARE AND
HIS STAGE

William Shakespeare was christened in Holy Trinity Church, Stratford-upon-Avon, April 26, 1564. His birth is traditionally assigned to April 23. He was the eldest of four boys and two girls who survived infancy in the family of John Shakespeare, glover and trader of Henley Street, and his wife Mary Arden, daughter of a small landowner of Wilmcote. In 1568 John was elected Bailiff (equivalent to Mayor) of Stratford, having already filled the minor municipal offices. The town maintained for the sons of the burgesses a free school, taught by a university graduate and offering preparation in Latin sufficient for university entrance; its early registers are lost, but there can be little doubt that Shakespeare received the formal part of his education in this school.

On November 27, 1582, a license was issued for the marriage of William Shakespeare (aged eighteen) and Ann Hathaway (aged twenty-six), and on May 26, 1583, their child Susanna was christened in Holy Trinity Church. The inference that the marriage was forced upon the youth is natural but not inevitable; betrothal was legally binding at the time, and was sometimes regarded as conferring conjugal rights. Two additional children of the marriage, the twins Hamnet and Judith, were christened on February 2, 1585. Meanwhile the prosperity of the elder Shakespeares had declined, and William was impelled to seek a career outside Stratford.

The tradition that he spent some time as a country

teacher is old but unverifiable. Because of the absence of records his early twenties are called the "lost years," and only one thing about them is certain – that at least some of these years were spent in winning a place in the acting profession. He may have begun as a provincial trouper, but by 1592 he was established in London and prominent enough to be attacked. In a pamphlet of that year, *Groats-worth of Wit*, the ailing Robert Greene complained of the neglect which university writers like himself had suffered from actors, one of whom was daring to set up as a playwright:

. . . an vpstart Crow, beautified with our feathers, that with his *Tygers hart wrapt in a Players hyde*, supposes he is as well able to bombast out a blanke verse as the best of you: and beeing an absolute *Iohannes fac totum*, is in his owne conceit the onely Shake-scene in a countrey.

The pun on his name, and the parody of his line "O tiger's heart wrapped in a woman's hide" (*3 Henry VI*), pointed clearly to Shakespeare. Some of his admirers protested, and Henry Chettle, the editor of Greene's pamphlet, saw fit to apologize:

. . . I am as sory as if the originall fault had beene my fault, because my selfe haue seene his demeanor no lesse ciuill than he excelent in the qualitie he professes: Besides, diuers of worship haue reported his vprightnes of dealing, which argues his honesty, and his facetious grace in writting, that approoues his Art. (Prefatory epistle, *Kind-Harts Dreame*)

The plague closed the London theatres for many months in 1592–94, denying the actors their livelihood. To this period belong Shakespeare's two narrative poems, *Venus and Adonis* and *The Rape of Lucrece*, both dedicated to the Earl of Southampton. No doubt the poet was rewarded with a gift of money as usual in such cases, but he did no further dedicating and we have no reliable information on whether Southampton, or anyone else, became his regular patron. His sonnets, first mentioned in 1598 and published without his consent in 1609, are intimate without being explicitly autobiographical. They seem to commemorate the poet's friendship with an idealized youth, rivalry with a more favored poet, and love affair with a dark mistress; and his bitterness when the mistress betrays him in conjunction with the friend; but it is difficult to decide precisely what the "story" is, impossible to decide whether it is fictional or true. The true distinction of the sonnets, at least of those not purely conventional, rests in the universality of the thoughts and moods they express, and in their poignancy and beauty.

In 1594 was formed the theatrical company known until 1603 as the Lord Chamberlain's men, thereafter as the King's men. Its original membership included, besides Shakespeare, the beloved clown Will Kempe and the famous actor Richard Burbage. The company acted in various London theatres and even toured the provinces, but it is chiefly associated in our minds with the Globe Theatre built on the south bank of the Thames in 1599. Shakespeare was an actor and joint owner of this company (and its Globe) through the remainder of his creative years. His plays, written at the average rate of two a year, together with Burbage's acting won it its place of leadership among the London companies.

Individual plays began to appear in print, in editions both honest and piratical, and the publishers became increasingly aware of the value of Shakespeare's name on the title pages. As early as 1598 he was hailed as the leading English dramatist in the *Palladis Tamia* of Francis Meres:

As *Plautus* and *Seneca* are accounted the best for Comedy and Tragedy among the Latines, so *Shakespeare* among the English is the most excellent in both kinds for the stage: for Comedy, witnes his *Gentlemen of Verona*, his *Errors*, his *Loue labors lost*, his *Loue labours wonne* [at one time in print but no longer extant, at least under this title], his *Midsummers night dream*, & his *Merchant of Venice*; for Tragedy, his *Richard the 2*, *Richard the 3*, *Henry the 4*, *King Iohn*, *Titus Andronicus*, and his *Romeo and Iuliet*.

The note is valuable both in indicating Shakespeare's prestige and in helping us to establish a chronology. In the second half of his writing career, history plays gave place to the great tragedies; and farces and light comedies gave place to the problem plays and symbolic romances. In 1623, seven years after his death, his former fellow-actors, John Heminge and Henry Condell, cooperated with a group of London printers in bringing out his plays in collected form. The volume is generally known as the First Folio.

Shakespeare had never severed his relations with Stratford. His wife and children may sometimes have shared his London lodgings, but their home was Stratford. His son Hamnet was buried there in 1596, and his daughters Susanna and Judith were married there in 1607 and 1616 respectively. (His father, for whom he had secured a coat of arms and thus the privilege of writing himself gentleman, died in 1601, his mother in 1608.) His considerable earnings in London, as actor-sharer, part owner of the Globe, and playwright, were invested chiefly in Stratford property. In 1597 he purchased for £60 New Place, one of the two most imposing residences in the town. A number of other business transactions, as well as minor episodes in his career, have left documentary records. By 1611 he was in a position to retire, and he seems gradually to have withdrawn from theatrical activity in order to live in Stratford. In March, 1616, he made a will, leaving token bequests to Burbage, Heminge, and Condell, but the bulk of his estate to his family. The most famous feature of the will, the bequest of the second-best bed to his wife, reveals nothing about Shakespeare's marriage; the quaintness of the provision seems commonplace to those familiar with ancient testaments. Shakespeare died April 23, 1616, and was buried in the Stratford church where he had been christened. Within seven years a monument was erected to his memory on the north wall of the chancel. Its portrait bust and the Droeshout engraving on the title page of the First Folio provide the only likenesses with an established claim to authenticity. The best verbal vignette was written by his rival Ben Jonson, the more impressive for being imbedded in a context mainly critical :

> ... I loved the man, and doe honour his memory (on this side idolatry) as much as any. Hee was indeed honest, and of an open and free nature: had an excellent Phantsie, brave notions, and gentle expressions.... (*Timber or Discoveries*, ca. 1623–30)

*

The reader of Shakespeare's plays is aided by a general knowledge of the way in which they were staged. The King's men acquired a roofed and artificially lighted theatre only toward the close of Shakespeare's career, and then only for winter use. Nearly all his plays were designed for performance in such structures as the Globe – a three-tiered amphitheatre with a large rectangular platform extending to the center of its yard. The plays were staged by daylight, by large casts brilliantly costumed, but with only a minimum of properties, without scenery, and quite possibly without intermissions. There was a rear stage gallery for action "above," and a curtained rear recess for "discoveries" and other special effects, but by far the major portion of any play was enacted upon the projecting platform, with episode following episode in swift succession, and with shifts of time and place signaled the audience only by the momentary clearing of the stage between the episodes. Information about the identity of the characters and, when necessary, about the time and place of the action was incorporated in the dialogue. No place-headings have been inserted in the present editions ; these are apt to obscure the original fluidity of structure, with the emphasis upon action and speech rather than scenic background. (Indications of place are supplied in the footnotes.) The acting, including that of the youthful apprentices to the profession who performed the parts of women, was highly skillful, with a premium placed upon grace of gesture and beauty of diction. The audiences, a cross section of the general public, commonly numbered a thousand, sometimes more than two thousand. Judged by the type of plays they applauded, these audiences were not only large but also perceptive.

THE TEXTS OF THE PLAYS

About half of Shakespeare's plays appeared in print for the first time in the folio volume of 1623. The others had been published individually, usually in quarto volumes, during his lifetime or in the six years following his death. The copy used by the printers of the quartos varied greatly in merit, sometimes representing Shakespeare's true text, sometimes only a debased version of that text. The copy used by the printers of the folio also varied in merit, but was chosen with care. Since it consisted of the best available manuscripts, or the more acceptable quartos (although frequently in editions other than the first), or of quartos corrected by reference to manuscripts, we have good or reasonably good texts of most of the thirty-seven plays.

In the present series, the plays have been newly edited from quarto or folio texts, depending, when a choice offered, upon which is now regarded by bibliographical specialists as the more authoritative. The ideal has been to reproduce the chosen texts with as few alterations as possible, beyond occasional relineation, expansion of abbreviations, and modernization of punctuation and spelling. Emendation is held to a minimum, and such material as has been added, in the way of stage directions and lines supplied by an alternative text, has been enclosed in square brackets.

None of the plays printed in Shakespeare's lifetime were divided into acts and scenes, and the inference is that the author's own manuscripts were not so divided. In the folio collection, some of the plays remained undivided, some were divided into acts, and some were divided into acts and scenes. During the eighteenth century all of the plays were divided into acts and scenes, and in the Cambridge edition of the mid-nineteenth century, from which the influential Globe text derived, this division was more or less regularized and the lines were numbered. Many useful works of reference employ the act–scene–line apparatus thus established.

Since this act–scene division is obviously convenient, but is of very dubious authority so far as Shakespeare's own structural principles are concerned, or the original manner of staging his plays, a problem is presented to modern editors. In the present series the act–scene division is retained marginally, and may be viewed as a reference aid like the line numbering. A star marks the points of division when these points have been determined by a cleared stage indicating a shift of time and place in the action of the play, or when no harm results from the editorial assumption that there is such a shift. However, at those points where the established division is clearly misleading – that is, where continuous action has been split up into separate "scenes" – the star is omitted and the distortion corrected. This mechanical expedient seemed the best means of combining utility and accuracy.

THE GENERAL EDITOR

INTRODUCTION

Critics have been known to speak of *Macbeth*, *King Lear*, and *Antony and Cleopatra* as Shakespeare's *Inferno*, *Purgatorio*, and *Paradiso*. The comparison is misleading if taken as a guide to Shakespeare's states of mind, of which we know nothing, or even as a guide to the order of the three plays, the consensus of modern opinion being that *Macbeth* (ca. 1606) falls between *King Lear* (ca. 1605) and *Antony and Cleopatra* (ca. 1607). But the notion has a certain merit if taken solely as a guide to tone.

Macbeth and *King Lear*, like *Othello* earlier, are dark plays, filled with actions taking place in what can only be called "dramatic" as well as literal night, a dark night of the soul engulfed by evil. *Antony and Cleopatra*, on the other hand, is a bright play. *Macbeth* and *King Lear*, too, are savage – if one fully responds to them, terrifying. There is no savagery in *Antony and Cleopatra*; it is moving, exhilarating, even exalting, but contains nothing that should tear an audience to tatters. The humor of *Macbeth* and *King Lear* is either grim or pitiful: a drunken porter at the gate of hell, a court jester shivering on a stormy heath. The humor of *Antony and Cleopatra* is neither grim nor pitiful, although sometimes acrid enough. Cleopatra is given qualities that make her a very unqueenly queen: she lies, wheedles, sulks, screams, and makes love, all with equal abandon. Antony is given qualities that make him in some senses more like an elderly playboy than a tragic hero. We are encouraged by Shakespeare in this play to

disengage ourselves from the protagonists, to feel superior
to them, even to laugh at them, as we rarely are with his
earlier tragic persons.

Against laughter, however, the playwright poises sym-
pathy and even admiration. Tawdry though he has made
these seasoned old campaigners in love and war, he has
also magnified and idealized them, to the point at which
their mutual passion becomes glorious as well as cheap.
Antony, the play tells us, has "infinite virtue," Cleopatra
"infinite variety." He is the "triple pillar of the world,"
she is the "day o' th' world." He seems a "plated Mars,"
she more beautiful than Venus. His guardian spirit is
called "unmatchable," she is called a "lass unparalleled."
He descends from the god Hercules, she from the moon-
goddess Isis. She sees him as the sun and moon, lighting
this "little O, th' earth"; Charmian sees her as the
"Eastern star." When Antony cries Ho! "Like boys unto
a muss, kings would start forth"; Cleopatra has a hand
that "kings Have lipped, and trembled kissing." When
Antony will swear an oath, he cries, "Let Rome in Tiber
melt and the wide arch Of the ranged empire fall!" When
Cleopatra will swear, she cries, "Melt Egypt into Nile!
and kindly creatures Turn all to serpents." Antony, about
to die, thinks of death as a continuing amour with
Cleopatra: "Where souls do couch on flowers, we'll hand
in hand, And with our sprightly port make the ghosts
gaze." When Cleopatra is about to die, she sees death in
the same transcendent terms: "Go fetch My best attires.
I am again for Cydnus, To meet Mark Antony."

Traces of Shakespeare's duality of attitude toward his
lovers may be found in Plutarch, whose *Lives of the Noble
Grecians and Romans Compared Together* he had read in
Thomas North's magnificent English rendering (1579) of
Jacques Amyot's translation of the original into French
(1559). So eloquent was North's prose that in certain
instances it could be assumed into blank verse with a
minimum of change, as in the following well-known

description of Cleopatra going to meet Antony in her barge, which should be compared with the lines of Enobarbus (II, ii, 191–241) in Shakespeare's play.

... She went to Antonius at the age when a woman's beauty is at the prime, and she also of best judgment. ... She disdained to set forward otherwise but to take her barge in the river of Cydnus, the poop whereof was of gold, the sails of purple, and the oars of silver, which kept stroke in rowing after the sound of the music of flutes, hautboys, cithers, viols, and such other instruments as they played upon in the barge. And now for the person of herself: She was laid under a pavilion of cloth-of-gold of tissue, apparelled and attired like the goddess Venus commonly drawn in picture; and hard by her, on either hand of her, pretty fair boys, apparelled as painters do set forth god Cupid, with little fans in their hands, with the which they fanned wind upon her. Her ladies and gentlewomen also, the fairest of them, were apparelled like the nymphs Nereides (which are the mermaids of the waters) and like the Graces, some steering the helm, others tending the tackle and ropes of the barge, out of the which there came a wonderful passing sweet savor of perfumes that perfumed the wharf's side, pestered with innumerable multitudes of people. Some of them followed the barge all alongest the river's side, others also ran out of the city to see her coming in, so that in the end there ran such multitudes of people one after another to see her that Antonius was left post-alone in the market place in his imperial seat to give audience. And there went a rumor in the people's mouths that the goddess Venus was come to play with the god Bacchus for the general good of all Asia.

Shakespeare's play owes to Plutarch's life of Antony many of its incidents, and to North's prose the wording of occasional passages like the lines of Enobarbus referred to above. It precipitates, however, an interpretation of these materials that is spectacularly Shakespeare's own. Plutarch's narrative, for all its stress on the baffling blends of vice and virtue in great minds, is at bottom the relatively familiar story of the Great Man and the Temptress. His Antony loses the world for love, not wisely but too well, and his Cleopatra, though possibly she rises to genuine love before the end (Plutarch leaves this point undecided), is rather the instrument of a great man's downfall than a tragic figure in herself. To understand the distinctiveness of Shakespeare's treatment of her, we have only to return to the passage in Plutarch and the lines of Enobarbus already cited. Plutarch's Cleopatra is all siren, every effect calculated to ensnare the senses of the conquering Roman. Shakespeare's Cleopatra is all siren too, but she is more. The repeated paradoxes in Enobarbus' language serve notice on us that everything about her is impossible, mysteriously contradictory. Her page-boys cool her cheeks only to make them burn, "and what they undid did." Her gentlewomen are seeming mermaids, half human, half sea-creature. The silken tackle swells with a life of its own at "the touches of those flower-soft hands." The wharves come alive and have "sense," quickened by her "strange invisible perfume." The city comes alive, to "cast" its people out upon her. Antony is left sitting in the market place, whistling to the air, and the air itself, except that nature abhors a vacuum, would have "gone to gaze on Cleopatra too" and left a gap behind. She is a creature, says Enobarbus in conclusion, who makes defect perfection, and, when breathless, power breathes forth. Other women cloy the appetites they feed, "but she makes hungry Where most she satisfies." Even the vilest things are so becoming when she does them that "the holy priests Bless her when she is riggish."

This is clearly not a portrait of a mere intriguing woman, but a kind of absolute oxymoron: Cleopatra is glimpsed here as a force like the Lucretian Venus, whose vitality resists both definition and regulation. Yet enveloped as she is by Enobarbus' mocking tones, wise and faintly world-weary, calculating amusedly the effects of his words on these uninitiated Romans, she remains the more a trollop for that. His reliable anti-romanticism undercuts the picture he draws of her, and at the same time confirms it, because it comes from him.

The ambiguity of these lines extends to almost everything in the play. In the world the dramatist has given his
lovers, nothing is stable, fixed, or sure, not even ultimate
values; all is in motion. Seen from one point of view, the
motion may be discerned as process, the inexorable march
of causes and effects, exemplified in Antony's fall and
epitomized by Caesar in commenting to Octavia on the
futility of her efforts to preserve the peace: "But let determined things to destiny Hold unbewailed their way."
Seen from another angle, the motion reveals itself as flux,
the restless waxing and waning of tides, of moons, of
human feeling. Especially of human feeling. Antony pursued Brutus to his death, we are reminded by Enobarbus,
yet wept when he found him slain. So within the play
itself Caesar weeps, having pursued Antony to his death;
and Antony, desiring that Fulvia die, finds her "good,
being gone"; and Enobarbus, seeking some way to leave
his master, is heart-struck when he succeeds; and the
Roman populace, always fickle, "Like to a vagabond flag
upon the stream, Goes to and back, lackeying the varying
tide, To rot itself with motion."

In such a context, it is not surprising that the lovers'
passion is subject to vicissitudes, going to and back in ever
more violent oscillations of attraction and recoil. Shakespeare nowhere disguises the unstable and ultimately
destructive character of their relationship, and those who,
like Shaw, have belabored him for not giving sexual
infatuation the satiric treatment it deserves have read too
carelessly. It is likewise not surprising that the play's
structure should reflect, in its abrupt and numerous shifts
of scene, so marked a quality of its leading characters –
their emotional and psychological vacillation. Though
these shifts have also met with criticism, some finding in
them a serious threat to unity, they are easily seen in the
theatre to be among the dramatist's means of conveying to
us an awareness of the competing values by which the
lovers, and particularly Antony, are torn. "Kingdoms are

clay," he declares in Egypt; "The nobleness of life Is to do
thus," and embraces Cleopatra. A few hours later, however, he says with equal earnestness, "These strong
Egyptian fetters I must break Or lose myself in dotage,"
and he departs for Rome. Again, he declares to Octavia in
Rome, hereafter everything shall "be done by th' rule,"
yet scarcely thirty lines later, after his interview with the
soothsayer, he has added, "I will to Egypt." From this
point on follows a succession of fluctuations in both war
and love. In war, confidence of victory shifting to despair
at loss, then to new confidence, then to new despair. In
love, adorings of Cleopatra changing to recriminations,
then to renewed adorings, then to fresh disgust. This aspect of the play's rhythm is vividly summed up in two
speeches in the third act (III, xi). "I have offended repu-
tation," Antony says after the first sea defeat, "A most un-
noble swerving": there is the voice of Rome and the
soldier. A few seconds after, he says to Cleopatra, "Fall
not a tear, I say: one of them rates All that is won and
lost": this is the voice of Egypt and the lover.

"All that is won *and* lost" is of course the crucial ambiguity of this tragedy. Perhaps it is one about which no
two readers are likely finally to agree. Much is obviously
lost by the lovers in the course of the play, and Shakespeare underscores this fact, as Plutarch had done, by
placing their deaths in Cleopatra's monument – that is
to say, a tomb. All those imperial ambitions that once
mustered the "kings o' th' earth for war" have shrunk
now to this narrow stronghold, which is also a waiting
grave. Antony had said as he put his arms about Cleopatra in the opening scene, "Here is my space." Now that
challenge has been taken up. This is his space indeed.

But what then, if anything, has been won? The answer
to this question depends as much on what one brings to
Antony and Cleopatra as on what one finds there, for the
evidence is mixed. Antony does give his life for his love
before the play ends, and we observe that there are no

recriminations at his final meeting with Cleopatra; only his quiet hope that she will remember him for what was noblest in him, and her acknowledgment that he was, and is, her man of men. But then, too, his death has been precipitated by her duplicity in the false report of hers; it has among its motives a self-interested desire to evade Caesar's triumph; and the suicide is even bungled in the doing: if this is a hero's death, it is a humiliating one. Likewise, Cleopatra seems to give her life for love. As Antony will be a bridegroom in his death, "and run into't As to a lover's bed," so Cleopatra will be a bride in hers, calling, "Husband, I come," receiving darkness as if it were "a lover's pinch, Which hurts, and is desired," and breathing out, in words that could equally be describing the union of life with death or the union of lover with lover, "As sweet as balm, as soft as air, as gentle – O Antony!" This, however, is the same woman who has long studied "easy ways to die," who ends her life only after becoming convinced that Caesar means to lead her in triumph, and who has cached away with her treasurer Seleucus more than half her valuables in case of need. True, the scene with Seleucus can be so played as to indicate that she is using his confession to dupe Caesar about her intention to die. But that is precisely the point. What the actor or reader makes of her conduct here will be conditioned by what he has made of her elsewhere, by what he makes of the play as a whole, and even, perhaps, by his beliefs about human nature and the depiction of human nature in art.

Are we to take the high-sounding phrases which introduce us to this remarkable love affair in the play's first scene as amorous rant?

CLEOPATRA
    If it be love indeed, tell me how much.
ANTONY
    There's beggary in the love that can be reckoned.

CLEOPATRA
I'll set a bourn how far to be beloved.
ANTONY
Then must thou needs find out new heaven, new earth.

Or is there a prophetic resonance in that reference to "new heaven, new earth," which we are meant to remember when Cleopatra, dreaming of a transcendent Antony –

His face was as the heav'ns, and therein stuck
A sun and moon, which kept their course and lighted
The little O, th' earth. . . .
His legs bestrid the ocean : his reared arm
Crested the world : his voice was propertied
As all the tunèd spheres –

consigns her baser elements to "baser life"? Does the passion of these two remain a destructive element to the bitter end, doomed like all the feeling in the play to "rot itself with motion"? Or, as the world slips from them, have they a glimmering of something they could not hav earlier understood, of another power besides death "Which shackles accidents and bolts up change"? Is it "paltry to be Caesar," as Cleopatra claims, since "Not being Fortune, he's but Fortune's knave"? Or is it more paltry to be Antony, and, as Caesar sees it, "give a kingdom for a mirth," as well as, eventually, the world?

To such questions, *Antony and Cleopatra*, like life itself, gives no clear-cut answers. Shakespeare holds the balance even, and does not decide for us who finally is the strumpet of the play, Antony's Cleopatra, or Caesar's Fortune, and who, therefore, is the "strumpet's fool." Those who would have it otherwise, who are "hot for certainties in this our life," as Meredith phrased it, should turn to other authors than Shakespeare, and should have been born into some other world than this.

Yale University   MAYNARD MACK

NOTE ON THE TEXT

Antony and Cleopatra was first published in the folio of 1623, in a
good text with full stage directions, evidently printed from Shakespeare's own draft after it had been prepared for stage production.
The folio text is undivided into acts and scenes. The division
appearing marginally in the present edition is editorial, and supplied only for reference purposes. The following list of departures
from the folio text, amplified from the one supplied by the editor,
perhaps errs on the side of inclusiveness; it omits only the most
obvious typographical errors, the instances of mislineation, and
the variations in speech-prefixes and proper names, including
several instances of "Cleopater" which may indicate an alternative
pronunciation. The adopted reading in italics is followed by the
folio reading in roman.

I, i, 18 *me !* me,   39 *On* One   50 *whose* who
I, ii, 4 *charge* change   37 *fertile* foretell   58 *Charmian* Alexas
   76 *Saw* Save   106 *minds* windes   108 s.d. Omitted (in F:
Enter another Messenger)   110 *1. Attendant* 1. Mes.   111
2. Attendant 2. Mes.   114 *Messenger* 3. Mes.   134 *occasion* an
occasion   175 *leave* love   180 *Hath* Have   189 *hair* heire
191 *place is* places   *requires* require
I, iii, 20 *What,* What   24 *know* – know.   25 *betrayed* betrayèd
   33 *sued* suèd   43 *services* Servicles   51 *thrived* thrivèd   80
blood : no more. blood no more ?   82 *my* (not in F)
I, iv, 3 *Our* One   8 *Vouchsafed* vouchsafe   9 *the abstract* th'
abstracts   21 *smell* smels   44 *deared* fear'd   46 *lackeying*
lacking   49 *Make* Makes   56 *wassails* Vassailes   75 *we* me
I, v, 5 *time* time :   29 *time?* time.   34 s.d. *Alexas* Alexas from
Caesar   50 *dumbed* dumbe   61 *man* mans
II, i, 41 *warred* wan'd   43 *greater.* greater,   44 *all,* all :
II, ii, 71–72 *you . . . Alexandria ;* you, . . . Alexandria   107 *soldier*
Souldier,   115–16 *staunch, . . . world* staunch . . . world :   120
so say   121 *reproof* proofe   122 *deserved* deservèd   146–47
hand : | Further hand / Further   171 s.d. *[Exeunt.]* Exit omnes.
   195 *lovesick with.* Love-sicke. | With   205 *glow* glove   207
gentlewomen Gentlewoman   224 *'no'* no   *heard* hard   229
ploughed ploughèd   233 *And, breathless,* And breathlesse
II, iii, 8 *Octavia* (not in F)   20 *high, unmatchable* high unmatchable   24 *thee, no more but when to thee.* thee no more but : when

to thee, 30 *away* alway

II, v, 10–11 *river : there,* | *My . . . off*, River there / My . . . off.
12 *finned* fine 28 *him,* him. 43 *is* 'tis 96 *face, to me* face to
me, 111 *Alexas;* Alexas 115 *not! – Charmian,* not Charmian,

II, vi, 19 *is* his 30 *present) how you take* present how you take)
43 *telling,* telling. 52 *gained* gainèd 58 *composition* compo-
sion 66 *meanings* meaning 69 *of* (not in F) 81 s.d. *Manent*
Manet

II, vii, 91 *is* he is 99 *grows* grow 101 *all four days* all, foure
dayes, 110 *bear* beate 119 *off* of 123 *Splits* Spleet's 127
father's Father 128–29 *not.* | *Menas* not Menas

III, i, 3 *body* body, 4 *army.* Army

III, ii, 10 *Agrippa* Ant. 16 *figures* Figure 20 *beetle.* [. . .] *So –*
Beetle, so : 49 *full* the full 59 *wept* weepe

III, iii, 21 *lookedst* look'st

III, iv, 8 *them* then 9 *took't* look't 24 *yours* your 30 *Your* You
38 *has* he's

III, v, 12 *world* would *hast* hadst *chaps,* chaps 14 *the one* (not
in F)

III, vi, 13 *he there proclaimed the kings* hither proclaimèd the King
19 *reported,* reported 22 *know* knowes 28 *triumvirate* Trium-
pherate 29 *being, that* being that, 78 *do* does

III, vii, 4 *it is* it it 5 *Is't not* If not, 23 *Toryne* Troine 35
muleters Militers 51 *Actium* Action 72 *Canidius* Ven. 78
Well Well,

III, x, s.d. *Enobarbus* Enobarbus and Scarus 14 *June* Inne 28
he his

III, xi, 19 *that* them 22 *pray,* pray 44 *He is* Hee's 47 *seize*
cease 56 *followed* followèd 58 *tow* stowe 59 *Thy* The

III, xiii, 10 *merèd* meered 55 *Caesar* Caesars 57 *feared* fearèd
60 *deserved* deservèd 74 *this :* this *deputation* disputation,
90 *me. Of late.* me of late. 103 *again. This* againe, the 112–13
eyes, | *In . . . filth* eyes / In . . . filth, 132 *'a* a 137 *whipped
for . . . him.* whipt. For . . . him, 162 *smite* smile 165 *discandying* discandering 168 *sits* sets 178 *sinewed* sinewèd
199 *on* in 201 s.d. *Exit* Exeunt

IV, i, 3 *combat,* combat.

IV, ii, 1 *No.* No ? 12 *And thou* Thou

IV, iii, 8 *4. Soldier* 2 10 *3. Soldier* 1 15 *loved* lovèd 17 *Omnes
(speak together)* Speak together. / Omnes.

IV, iv, 5–6 *too.* | *What's* too, Anthony. | What's 6 *Antony* (not in
F) 8 *Cleopatra* (not in F) 24 *Captain* Alex. 32 *thee* thee.
33 *steel*. Steele,

IV, v, 1, 3, 6 *Soldier* Eros 17 *Dispatch*. Dispatch

IV, vi, 20 *more* mote 36 *do't, I feel*. doo't. I feele

IV, vii, 8 s.d. *far off* (in F after 'heads', line 6)

IV, viii, 18 *My* Mine 23 *favoring* savouring 26 *Destroyed*
Destroyèd

IV, xii, 4 *augurers* Auguries 9 s.d. *Alarum . . . sea-fight* (in F
before line 1) 10 *betrayed* betrayèd 21 *spanieled* pannelled

IV, xiii, 10 *death*. death

IV, xiv, 4 *towered* toward 10 *dislimns* dislimes 19 *Caesar*
Caesars 77 *ensued* ensuèd 95 s.d. *Kills himself* (in F after
line 93) 104 *ho* how

IV, xv, 54 *lived the* lived. The 76 *e'en* in 86 *What, what !* What,
what

V, i, s.d. *Maecenas* Menas 28 *Agrippa* Dol. 31 *Agrippa* Dola.
36 *followed* followèd 48 s.d. *Enter an Egyptian* (in F after
'says', line 51) 53 *all she has*, all, she has 54 *intents desires*
intents, desires, 59 *live* leave 68 s.d. *Exit* Exit Proculeius

V, ii, 35 *You* Pro. [s.p.] You 56 *varletry* Varlotarie 66 *me* (not
in F) 81 *O*, o' 87 *autumn 'twas* Anthony it was 104 *smites*
suites 139 *valued* valewèd 151 *followed* followèd 216 *Ballad us out o'* Ballads us out a 223 *my* mine 317 *awry* away
318 s.d. *in.* in, and Dolabella. 324 *here !* Charmian here
Charmian 340 *diadem* diadem; 341 *mistress ;* Mistris

ANTONY
AND CLEOPATRA

Mark Antony ⎱
Octavius Caesar ⎰ triumvirs
M. Aemilius Lepidus ⎰
Sextus Pompeius
Domitius Enobarbus ⎫
Ventidius
Eros
Scarus ⎬ friends to Antony
Decretas
Demetrius
Philo ⎭
Canidius, lieutenant-general to Antony
Maecenas ⎫
Agrippa
Dolabella
Proculeius ⎬ friends to Caesar
Thidias
Gallus ⎭
Taurus, lieutenant-general to Caesar
Menas ⎱
Menecrates ⎬ friends to Pompey
Varrius ⎰
Roman Officer under Ventidius
A Schoolmaster, ambassador from Antony to Caesar
Alexas ⎫
Mardian
Seleucus ⎬ attendants on Cleopatra
Diomedes ⎭
A Soothsayer
A Clown
Cleopatra, Queen of Egypt
Octavia, sister to Caesar and wife to Antony
Charmian ⎱
Iras ⎰ attendants on Cleopatra
Officers, Soldiers, Messengers, Attendants

Scene : The Roman Empire]

ANTONY
AND CLEOPATRA

Enter Demetrius and Philo.   I, i

PHILO

Nay, but this dotage of our general's   1
O'erflows the measure : those his goodly eyes
That o'er the files and musters of the war
Have glowed like plated Mars, now bend, now turn   4
The office and devotion of their view   5
Upon a tawny front. His captain's heart,   6
Which in the scuffles of great fights hath burst
The buckles on his breast, reneges all temper   8
And is become the bellows and the fan
To cool a gypsy's lust.   10

    *Flourish. Enter Antony, Cleopatra, her Ladies, the
    Train, with Eunuchs fanning her.*

                Look where they come :
Take but good note, and you shall see in him
The triple pillar of the world transformed   12
Into a strumpet's fool. Behold and see.   13

CLEOPATRA

If it be love indeed, tell me how much.

I, i The palace of Cleopatra in Alexandria   1 *dotage* (applicable not only
to the aged; Antony 'dotes' on Cleopatra)   4 *plated* armored   5 *office*
service   6 *front* face (with pun on military sense)   8 *reneges* rejects;
temper moderation   10 *gypsy* (1) native of Egypt (gypsies were thought to
originate thence), (2) slut   12 *The triple . . . world* one of the three 'pillars'
of the world (the others being Octavius Caesar and Lepidus)   13 *fool*
dupe

ANTONY
There's beggary in the love that can be reckoned.

CLEOPATRA
16   I'll set a bourn how far to be beloved.

ANTONY
Then must thou needs find out new heaven, new earth.
Enter a Messenger.

MESSENGER
News my good lord, from Rome.

18 **ANTONY**   Grates me ! The sum.

CLEOPATRA
Nay, hear them, Antony.

20   Fulvia perchance is angry ; or who knows
21   If the scarce-bearded Caesar have not sent
His pow'rful mandate to you, 'Do this, or this ;
23   Take in that kingdom, and enfranchise that.
Perform't, or else we damn thee.'

ANTONY   How, my love ?

CLEOPATRA
Perchance ? Nay, and most like :
26   You must not stay here longer, your dismission
Is come from Caesar ; therefore hear it, Antony.
28   Where's Fulvia's process ? Caesar's I would say ? both ?
Call in the messengers. As I am Egypt's Queen,
Thou blushest, Antony, and that blood of thine
31   Is Caesar's homager : else so thy cheek pays shame
When shrill-tongued Fulvia scolds. The messengers !

ANTONY
Let Rome in Tiber melt and the wide arch
34   Of the ranged empire fall ! Here is my space,
Kingdoms are clay : our dungy earth alike

---

16 *bourn* limit   18 *Grates . . . sum* it annoys me; be brief   20 *Fulvia*
Antony's wife   21 *scarce-bearded* hardly grown up (Octavius was twenty-
three)   23 *Take in* seize; *enfranchise* set free   26 *dismission* recall   28
process summons   31 *Is Caesar's homager* pays respect to Caesar's
authority; *else* or else   34 *ranged* well-ordered (?), wide-ranging (?)

  Feeds beast as man. The nobleness of life
  Is to do thus; when such a mutual pair 37
  And such a twain can do't, in which I bind,
  On pain of punishment, the world to weet 39
  We stand up peerless.
CLEOPATRA   Excellent falsehood!
  Why did he marry Fulvia, and not love her?
  I'll seem the fool I am not. Antony 42
  Will be himself.
ANTONY   But stirred by Cleopatra.
  Now for the love of Love and her soft hours,
  Let's not confound the time with conference harsh. 45
  There's not a minute of our lives should stretch 46
  Without some pleasure now. What sport to-night?
CLEOPATRA
  Hear the ambassadors.
ANTONY   Fie, wrangling queen!
  Whom every thing becomes – to chide, to laugh,
  To weep; whose every passion fully strives 50
  To make itself, in thee, fair and admired.
  No messenger but thine, and all alone
  To-night we'll wander through the streets and note
  The qualities of people. Come, my queen;
  Last night you did desire it. – Speak not to us.
    Exeunt [Antony and Cleopatra] with the Train.
DEMETRIUS
  Is Caesar with Antonius prized so slight? 56
PHILO
  Sir, sometimes when he is not Antony
  He comes too short of that great property 58
  Which still should go with Antony.
DEMETRIUS   I am full sorry

---

37 *thus* (perhaps indicating an embrace; perhaps a general reference to their way of life) 39 *weet* know 42 *the fool ... not* i.e. foolish enough to believe you 45 *confound* destroy, waste 46 *stretch* pass 50 *passion* mood 56 *prized* valued 58 *property* distinction

60 That he approves the common liar, who
    Thus speaks of him at Rome; but I will hope
    Of better deeds to-morrow. Rest you happy!   *Exeunt.*

                            *

I, ii   *Enter Enobarbus, Lamprius, a Soothsayer, Rannius,*
          Lucillius, Charmian, Iras, Mardian the Eunuch, and
          Alexas.

CHARMIAN Lord Alexas, sweet Alexas, most anything
2   Alexas, almost most absolute Alexas, where's the sooth-
    sayer that you praised so to th' Queen? O that I knew
4   this husband which, you say, must charge his horns
    with garlands!

ALEXAS Soothsayer!

SOOTHSAYER Your will?

CHARMIAN Is this the man? Is't you, sir, that know
    things?

SOOTHSAYER
    In nature's infinite book of secrecy
    A little I can read.

ALEXAS Show him your hand.

ENOBARBUS
    Bring in the banquet quickly: wine enough
    Cleopatra's health to drink.

CHARMIAN Good sir, give me good fortune.

SOOTHSAYER
    I make not, but foresee.

CHARMIAN Pray then, foresee me one.

---

60 *approves* confirms
I, ii The chambers of Cleopatra   s.d. *Enter Enobarbus . . . Alexas* (thus in
folio, but Lamprius, Rannius, and Lucillius do not speak in the scene and
do not appear elsewhere in the play. Possibly Lamprius is the name of the
Soothsayer.)   **2** *absolute* perfect   **4–5** *must . . . garlands* i.e. must be not
only a cuckold and grow horns (as cuckolds – husbands of unfaithful
wives – were humorously said to do) but a champion cuckold, wearing a
winner's garland

SOOTHSAYER
  You shall be yet far fairer than you are.

CHARMIAN He means in flesh.   17

IRAS No, you shall paint when you are old.

CHARMIAN Wrinkles forbid!

ALEXAS Vex not his prescience, be attentive.

CHARMIAN Hush!

SOOTHSAYER
  You shall be more beloving than beloved.

CHARMIAN I had rather heat my liver with drinking.   23

ALEXAS Nay, hear him.

CHARMIAN Good now, some excellent fortune. Let me
  be married to three kings in a forenoon and widow them
  all. Let me have a child at fifty, to whom Herod of Jewry   27
  may do homage. Find me to marry me with Octavius
  Caesar, and companion me with my mistress.   ̃9

SOOTHSAYER
  You shall outlive the lady whom you serve.

CHARMIAN O excellent! I love long life better than figs.

SOOTHSAYER
  You have seen and proved a fairer former fortune   32
  Than that which is to approach.

CHARMIAN Then belike my children shall have no names.   34
  Prithee, how many boys and wenches must I have?   35

SOOTHSAYER
  If every of your wishes had a womb,
  And fertile every wish, a million.

CHARMIAN Out, fool! I forgive thee for a witch.   38

ALEXAS You think none but your sheets are privy to your   39
  wishes.

---

17 *He . . . flesh* he means that you will put on weight   23 *heat . . . drinking*
i.e. rather than with unreciprocated love (the liver being regarded as love's
residence)   27–28 *to . . . homage* i.e. to whom even King Herod (who
massacred the infants of Judea) would do homage   29 *companion me with*
give me as my servant   32 *proved* experienced   34 *have no names* be
illegitimate   35 *wenches* girls   38 *I . . . witch* i.e. I can see that you have no
prophetic powers   39 *privy to* in on the secret of

CHARMIAN Nay, come, tell Iras hers.

ALEXAS We'll know all our fortunes.

ENOBARBUS Mine, and most of our fortunes, to-night, shall be – drunk to bed.

IRAS There's a palm presages chastity, if nothing else.

CHARMIAN E'en as the o'erflowing Nilus presageth famine.

IRAS Go, you wild bedfellow, you cannot soothsay.

48 CHARMIAN Nay, if an oily palm be not a fruitful prognostication, I cannot scratch mine ear. Prithee tell her
50 but a workyday fortune.

SOOTHSAYER Your fortunes are alike.

IRAS But how, but how? Give me particulars.

SOOTHSAYER I have said.

IRAS Am I not an inch of fortune better than she?

CHARMIAN Well, if you were but an inch of fortune better than I, where would you choose it?

IRAS Not in my husband's nose.

CHARMIAN Our worser thoughts Heavens mend! Alexas – come, his fortune, his fortune. O, let him marry a
60 woman that cannot go, sweet Isis, I beseech thee, and let her die too, and give him a worse, and let worse follow worse till the worst of all follow him laughing to his grave, fiftyfold a cuckold. Good Isis, hear me this prayer, though thou deny me a matter of more weight: good Isis, I beseech thee.

IRAS Amen, dear goddess, hear that prayer of the people.
67 For, as it is a heartbreaking to see a handsome man loose-wived, so it is a deadly sorrow to behold a foul knave
69 uncuckolded. Therefore, dear Isis, keep decorum, and fortune him accordingly.

CHARMIAN Amen.

---

48 *oily palm* (symptom of sensuality); *fruitful prognostication* prophetic sign of fertility   **50** *workyday* ordinary   **60** *go* bear children (?), give – or receive – sexual satisfaction (?); *Isis* Egyptian goddess of earth, fertility, and the moon   **67** *loose-wived* married to a loose woman   **69** *keep decorum* i.e. act as suits his quality

ALEXAS Lo now, if it lay in their hands to make me a
cuckold, they would make themselves whores but
they'ld do't.   74
    Enter Cleopatra.

ENOBARBUS
  Hush, here comes Antony.
CHARMIAN   Not he, the Queen.
CLEOPATRA
  Saw you my lord?
ENOBARBUS   No, lady.
CLEOPATRA   Was he not here?
CHARMIAN No, madam.
CLEOPATRA
  He was disposed to mirth; but on the sudden
  A Roman thought hath struck him. Enobarbus!
ENOBARBUS Madam?
CLEOPATRA
  Seek him, and bring him hither. Where's Alexas?
ALEXAS
  Here at your service. My lord approaches.
    Enter Antony with a Messenger [and Attendants].
CLEOPATRA
  We will not look upon him. Go with us.
        Exeunt [all but Antony, Messenger,
                and Attendants].
MESSENGER
  Fulvia thy wife first came into the field.
ANTONY
  Against my brother Lucius?
MESSENGER Ay.
  But soon that war had end, and the time's state   87
  Made friends of them, jointing their force 'gainst Caesar,

---

74 s.d. (this, the folio's, placing of Cleopatra's entrance suggests either that
the sound of her approach is heard before she can be seen, thus causing
Enobarbus' error, or that his remark is ironical, alluding to her power over
Antony's will)   87 *time's state* conditions of the moment

89   Whose better issue in the war from Italy
90   Upon the first encounter drave them.

ANTONY   Well, what worst?

MESSENGER
The nature of bad news infects the teller.

ANTONY
When it concerns the fool or coward. On.
Things that are past are done with me. 'Tis thus:
Who tells me true, though in his tale lie death,
95   I hear him as he flattered.

MESSENGER   Labienus
(This is stiff news) hath with his Parthian force
97   Extended Asia: from Euphrates,
His conquering banner shook, from Syria
To Lydia and to Ionia,
Whilst –

ANTONY Antony, thou wouldst say.

MESSENGER   O, my lord.

ANTONY
101   Speak to me home, mince not the general tongue,
Name Cleopatra as she is called in Rome:
Rail thou in Fulvia's phrase, and taunt my faults
104   With such full license as both truth and malice
Have power to utter. O, then we bring forth weeds
106   When our quick minds lie still, and our ills told us
107   Is as our earing. Fare thee well awhile.

MESSENGER
At your noble pleasure.   *Exit Messenger.*

ANTONY
From Sicyon, how the news? Speak there!

1. ATTENDANT
The man from Sicyon – is there such an one?

---

89 *issue* success   90 *drave* drove   95 *as* as if; *Labienus* Quintus Labienus,
who had been sent by Brutus and Cassius to seek aid against Antony and
Octavius Caesar from Orodes, King of Parthia, and was now commanding
a Parthian army   97 *Extended* seized   101 *home* plainly; *mince . . . tongue*
don't soften what everybody is saying   104 *license* freedom   106 *quick*
live, fertile   107 *earing* being ploughed (to uproot the weeds)

2. ATTENDANT
He stays upon your will.   111
ANTONY   Let him appear.
These strong Egyptian fetters I must break
Or lose myself in dotage.
          Enter another Messenger, with a letter.
                              What are you?
MESSENGER
Fulvia thy wife is dead.
ANTONY   Where died she?
MESSENGER
In Sicyon.
Her length of sickness, with what else more serious
Importeth thee to know, this bears.   117
          [Gives a letter.]
ANTONY   Forbear me.
                              [Exit Messenger.]
There's a great spirit gone! Thus did I desire it:
What our contempts doth often hurl from us,
We wish it ours again. The present pleasure,
By revolution low'ring, does become   121
The opposite of itself: she's good, being gone;
The hand could pluck her back that shoved her on.
I must from this enchanting queen break off: 124
Ten thousand harms, more than the ills I know,
My idleness doth hatch.   126
          Enter Enobarbus.
How now, Enobarbus!
ENOBARBUS What's your pleasure, sir?
ANTONY I must with haste from hence.
ENOBARBUS Why, then we kill all our women. We see
   how mortal an unkindness is to them. If they suffer our
   departure, death's the word.

---

111 *stays upon* awaits 117 *Importeth* concerns; *Forbear* leave 121 *By
revolution low'ring* i.e. moving downward on the revolving wheel of our
opinions 124 *enchanting* (Cleopatra is felt by the Romans in the play to
have witchlike powers of seduction) 126 *idleness* trifling

ANTONY I must be gone.

ENOBARBUS Under a compelling occasion let women die.
It were pity to cast them away for nothing, though
between them and a great cause they should be es-
teemed nothing. Cleopatra, catching but the least noise
of this, dies instantly: I have seen her die twenty times
139   upon far poorer moment. I do think there is mettle in
death, which commits some loving act upon her, she
hath such a celerity in dying.

ANTONY She is cunning past man's thought.

ENOBARBUS Alack, sir, no; her passions are made of
nothing but the finest part of pure love. We cannot call
her winds and waters sighs and tears: they are greater
storms and tempests than almanacs can report. This
147   cannot be cunning in her; if it be, she makes a shower of
148   rain as well as Jove.

ANTONY Would I had never seen her!

ENOBARBUS O, sir, you had then left unseen a wonderful
piece of work, which not to have been blest withal
would have discredited your travel.

ANTONY Fulvia is dead.

ENOBARBUS Sir?

ANTONY Fulvia is dead.

ENOBARBUS Fulvia?

ANTONY Dead.

ENOBARBUS Why, sir, give the gods a thankful sacrifice.
When it pleaseth their deities to take the wife of a man
160   from him, it shows to man the tailors of the earth;
comforting therein, that when old robes are worn out,
there are members to make new. If there were no more
163   women but Fulvia, then had you indeed a cut, and the
164   case to be lamented. This grief is crowned with consola-
tion, your old smock brings forth a new petticoat, and

---

139 *moment* cause; *mettle* vigor   147 *makes* manufactures   148 *Jove* i.e.
Jupiter Pluvius, Roman god of rain   160 *the tailors* i.e. that the gods are
the tailors   163, 164, 169 (in *cut, case, business,* and *broached,* Enobarbus
puns bawdily)

indeed the tears live in an onion that should water this
sorrow.

ANTONY

The business she hath broachèd in the state   167
Cannot endure my absence.

ENOBARBUS And the business you have broached here 169
cannot be without you; especially that of Cleopatra's,
which wholly depends on your abode.   171

ANTONY

No more light answers. Let our officers
Have notice what we purpose. I shall break   173
The cause of our expedience to the Queen   174
And get her leave to part. For not alone
The death of Fulvia, with more urgent touches,   176
Do strongly speak to us, but the letters too
Of many our contriving friends in Rome   178
Petition us at home. Sextus Pompeius   179
Hath given the dare to Caesar and commands
The empire of the sea. Our slippery people,
Whose love is never linked to the deserver
Till his deserts are past, begin to throw   183
Pompey the Great and all his dignities
Upon his son; who, high in name and power,
Higher than both in blood and life, stands up   186
For the main soldier; whose quality, going on,   187
The sides o' th' world may danger. Much is breeding,   188
Which, like the courser's hair, hath yet but life   189
And not a serpent's poison. Say, our pleasure,

---

167 *broachèd* opened up   **169** (see 163n.)   **171** *abode* staying   **173** *break*
tell   **174** *expedience* haste   **176** *touches* motives   **178** *contriving* i.e.
acting in my interest   **179** *at home* to return home; *Sextus Pompeius* son
of Pompey the Great, who had been outlawed, but, owing to the division
between Antony and Octavius Caesar, was able to seize Sicily and command
the Roman sea-routes   **183** *throw* transfer   **186** *blood and life* vital energy
187 *quality* character and position; *going on* evolving   **188** *danger* en-
danger   **189** *courser's hair* (horse hairs in water were thought to come to
life as small serpents)

191 To such whose place is under us, requires
Our quick remove from hence.
ENOBARBUS I shall do't. *[Exeunt.]*

*

I, iii   *Enter Cleopatra, Charmian, Alexas, and Iras.*

CLEOPATRA
Where is he?
CHARMIAN   I did not see him since.
CLEOPATRA
See where he is, who's with him, what he does:
3   I did not send you. If you find him sad,
Say I am dancing; if in mirth, report
That I am sudden sick. Quick, and return. *[Exit Alexas.]*
CHARMIAN
Madam, methinks, if you did love him dearly,
You do not hold the method to enforce
The like from him.
8 CLEOPATRA   What should I do, I do not?
CHARMIAN
In each thing give him way, cross him in nothing.
CLEOPATRA
Thou teachest like a fool: the way to lose him!
CHARMIAN
11   Tempt him not so too far. I wish, forbear.
In time we hate that which we often fear.
    Enter Antony.
But here comes Antony.
CLEOPATRA   I am sick and sullen.
ANTONY
14   I am sorry to give breathing to my purpose –
CLEOPATRA
Help me away, dear Charmian! I shall fall.

191 *place* rank
I, iii The chambers of Cleopatra   3 *sad* serious   8 *I do not* that I am not
doing   11 *Tempt* try; *I wish* I wish you would   14 *breathing* utterance

It cannot be thus long ; the sides of nature   16
Will not sustain it.

ANTONY   Now, my dearest queen –

CLEOPATRA
Pray you stand farther from me.

ANTONY   What's the matter ?

CLEOPATRA
I know by that same eye there's some good news.
What, says the married woman you may go ?   20
Would she had never given you leave to come !
Let her not say 'tis I that keep you here.
I have no power upon you : hers you are.

ANTONY
The gods best know –

CLEOPATRA   O, never was there queen
So mightily betrayed : yet at the first
I saw the treasons planted.

ANTONY   Cleopatra –

CLEOPATRA
Why should I think you can be mine, and true,
(Though you in swearing shake the thronèd gods)
Who have been false to Fulvia ? Riotous madness,
To be entangled with those mouth-made vows
Which break themselves in swearing.

ANTONY   Most sweet queen –

CLEOPATRA
Nay, pray you seek no color for your going,   32
But bid farewell, and go : when you sued staying,   33
Then was the time for words : no going then,
Eternity was in our lips and eyes,
Bliss in our brows' bent : none our parts so poor   36
But was a race of heaven. They are so still,   37
Or thou, the greatest soldier of the world,
Art turned the greatest liar.

16 *sides of nature* human body   20 *the married woman* i.e. Fulvia   32 *color*
pretext   33 *sued* begged for   36 *bent* curve   37 *a race of heaven* of
heavenly origin (?), of heavenly flavor (?)

ANTONY   How now, lady?
CLEOPATRA
    I would I had thy inches; thou shouldst know
41   There were a heart in Egypt.
ANTONY   Hear me, Queen:
    The strong necessity of time commands
    Our services awhile, but my full heart
44   Remains in use with you. Our Italy
45   Shines o'er with civil swords; Sextus Pompeius
    Makes his approaches to the port of Rome;
    Equality of two domestic powers
48   Breed scrupulous faction; the hated, grown to strength,
    Are newly grown to love; the condemned Pompey,
    Rich in his father's honor, creeps apace
    Into the hearts of such as have not thrived
52   Upon the present state, whose numbers threaten;
53   And quietness, grown sick of rest, would purge
54   By any desperate change. My more particular,
55   And that which most with you should safe my going,
    Is Fulvia's death.
CLEOPATRA
    Though age from folly could not give me freedom,
    It does from childishness. Can Fulvia die?
ANTONY
    She's dead, my queen.
    Look here, and at thy sovereign leisure read
61   The garboils she awaked. At the last, best,
    See when and where she died.
CLEOPATRA   O most false love!
63   Where be the sacred vials thou shouldst fill
    With sorrowful water? Now I see, I see,
    In Fulvia's death, how mine received shall be.

41 *Egypt* Cleopatra 44 *in . . . you* for you to keep and use 45 *civil swords*
i.e. civil war 48 *scrupulous faction* contest over trifles 52 *state* government
53–54 *grown . . . change* i.e. ill through peace, would cure itself by letting
blood 54 *particular* personal concern 55 *safe* make safe 61 *garboils*
commotions; *best* best news of all 63–64 *sacred vials . . . water* (a reference
to the practice of consecrating bottles of tears to the dead)

ANTONY
Quarrel no more, but be prepared to know
The purposes I bear : which are, or cease,
As you shall give th' advice. By the fire   68
That quickens Nilus' slime, I go from hence   69
Thy soldier, servant, making peace or war
As thou affects.   71
CLEOPATRA   Cut my lace, Charmian, come ;
But let it be, I am quickly ill, and well –
So Antony loves.   73
ANTONY   My precious queen, forbear,
And give true evidence to his love, which stands   74
An honorable trial.
CLEOPATRA   So Fulvia told me.   75
I prithee turn aside and weep for her ;
Then bid adieu to me, and say the tears
Belong to Egypt. Good now, play one scene
Of excellent dissembling, and let it look,
Like perfect honor.
ANTONY   You'll heat my blood : no more.
CLEOPATRA
You can do better yet ; but this is meetly.   81
ANTONY
Now by my sword –
CLEOPATRA   And target. Still he mends.   82
But this is not the best. Look, prithee, Charmian,
How this Herculean Roman does become   84
The carriage of his chafe.
ANTONY
I'll leave you, lady.
CLEOPATRA   Courteous lord, one word.

---

68 *fire* i.e. the sun   69 *quickens* vivifies ; *Nilus' slime* fertile mud left by the
Nile's annual overflow   71 *affects* choosest ; *lace* i.e. of her bodice   73 *So*
provided (?), with sudden changes like my own change now (?) ; *forbear*
desist   74 *stands* will sustain   75 *told* taught (through my observing how
faithful you were to her)   81 *meetly* well suited to the occasion   82 *target*
shield   84–85 *How . . . chafe* i.e. how becomingly he plays his role of angry
Hercules (from whom Antony was supposed to be descended)

Sir, you and I must part, but that's not it :
Sir, you and I have loved, but there's not it :
That you know well. Something it is I would –
90 O, my oblivion is a very Antony,
91 And I am all forgotten.

ANTONY   But that your royalty
Holds idleness your subject, I should take you
For idleness itself.

CLEOPATRA   'Tis sweating labor
To bear such idleness so near the heart
As Cleopatra this. But, sir, forgive me,
96 Since my becomings kill me when they do not
97 Eye well to you. Your honor calls you hence ;
Therefore be deaf to my unpitied folly,
And all the gods go with you. Upon your sword
Sit laurel victory, and smooth success
Be strewed before your feet !

ANTONY   Let us go. Come :
Our separation so abides and flies
That thou residing here goes yet with me,
And I hence fleeting here remain with thee.
Away !   *Exeunt.*

*

I, iv   *Enter Octavius [Caesar], reading a letter, Lepidus,*
           and their Train.

CAESAR
You may see, Lepidus, and henceforth know
It is not Caesar's natural vice to hate
3 Our great competitor. From Alexandria
This is the news : he fishes, drinks, and wastes
The lamps of night in revel ; is not more manlike

90 *my . . . Antony* my forgetfulness is like Antony, who is now leaving, i.e.
forgetting, me   91 *I . . . forgotten* (1) I have forgotten what I was going to
say, (2) I am all forgotten by Antony   91–92 *But . . . subject* if you were not
the queen of trifling   96 *my becomings* the emotions that become me (in
my situation of abandoned lover)   97 *Eye* look
I, iv The house of Octavius Caesar in Rome   3 *competitor* partner

Than Cleopatra, nor the queen of Ptolemy   6
More womanly than he; hardly gave audience, or   7
Vouchsafed to think he had partners. You shall find there
A man who is the abstract of all faults   9
That all men follow.

LEPIDUS   I must not think there are
Evils enow to darken all his goodness: 11
His faults, in him, seem as the spots of heaven,   12
More fiery by night's blackness; hereditary
Rather than purchased, what he cannot change   14
Than what he chooses.

CAESAR
You are too indulgent. Let's grant it is not
Amiss to tumble on the bed of Ptolemy,
To give a kingdom for a mirth, to sit
And keep the turn of tippling with a slave,   19
To reel the streets at noon, and stand the buffet   20
With knaves that smell of sweat. Say this becomes him
(As his composure must be rare indeed   22
Whom these things cannot blemish), yet must Antony
No way excuse his foils when we do bear   24
So great weight in his lightness. If he filled
His vacancy with his voluptuousness,   26
Full surfeits and the dryness of his bones   27
Call on him for't. But to confound such time   28
That drums him from his sport and speaks as loud   29
As his own state and ours, 'tis to be chid
As we rate boys who, being mature in knowledge,   31

6 *Ptolemy* Cleopatra's dead husband   7 *audience* i.e. to Caesar's messengers
(cf. I, i)   9 *is the abstract of* sums up   11 *enow* enough   12–13 *His* . . .
blackness i.e. like stars that show the brighter by night's blackness, Antony's
faults stand out the more in the present dark political situation   14
purchased acquired   19 *keep* . . . *of* take turns   20 *stand the buffet* trade
blows   22 *his composure* that man's make-up   24 *foils* disgraces   24–25
when . . . *lightness* when his levity puts so heavy a burden upon us   26
vacancy leisure   27–28 *Full* . . . *him* i.e. let his own physical symptoms be
the reckoning   28 *confound* destroy, waste   29–30 *speaks* . . . *ours* calls
urgently for decisions affecting the political futures of all of us   31 *rate*
berate; *mature in knowledge* old enough to know better

Pawn their experience to their present pleasure
33 And so rebel to judgment.
    Enter a Messenger.
LEPIDUS   Here's more news.
MESSENGER
Thy biddings have been done, and every hour,
Most noble Caesar, shalt thou have report
How 'tis abroad. Pompey is strong at sea,
And it appears he is beloved of those
That only have feared Caesar : to the ports
39 The discontents repair, and men's reports
40 Give him much wronged.
   CAESAR   I should have known no less.
41 It hath been taught us from the primal state
That he which is was wished until he were ;
And the ebbed man, ne'er loved till ne'er worth love,
44 Comes deared by being lacked. This common body,
45 Like to a vagabond flag upon the stream,
46 Goes to and back, lackeying the varying tide,
To rot itself with motion.
MESSENGER   Caesar, I bring thee word
Menecrates and Menas, famous pirates,
Make the sea serve them, which they ear and wound
With keels of every kind. Many hot inroads
They make in Italy ; the borders maritime
52 Lack blood to think on't, and flush youth revolt.
No vessel can peep forth but 'tis as soon
54 Taken as seen ; for Pompey's name strikes more
Than could his war resisted.
CAESAR   Antony,
56 Leave thy lascivious wassails. When thou once
Was beaten from Modena, where thou slew'st

33 *to judgment* against good sense 39 *discontents* discontented 40 *Give*
declare 41 *from . . . state* since government began 44 *Comes deared*
becomes beloved; *common body* common people 45 *flag* iris 46 *lackeying*
following obsequiously 52 *Lack blood* grow pale; *flush* vigorous 54–55
strikes . . . resisted is more effective than his forces would be if opposed
56 *wassails* carousings

Hirtius and Pansa, consuls, at thy heel
Did famine follow, whom thou fought'st against
(Though daintily brought up) with patience more
Than savages could suffer. Thou didst drink
The stale of horses and the gilded puddle   62
Which beasts would cough at. Thy palate then did deign
The roughest berry on the rudest hedge.
Yea, like the stag when snow the pasture sheets,
The barks of trees thou browsed. On the Alps
It is reported thou didst eat strange flesh,
Which some did die to look on. And all this
(It wounds thine honor that I speak it now)
Was borne so like a soldier that thy cheek
So much as lanked not.   71
LEPIDUS   'Tis pity of him.
CAESAR
  Let his shames quickly
  Drive him to Rome. 'Tis time we twain
  Did show ourselves i' th' field ; and to that end
  Assemble we immediate council. Pompey
  Thrives in our idleness.
LEPIDUS   To-morrow, Caesar,
  I shall be furnished to inform you rightly
  Both what by sea and land I can be able   78
  To front this present time.   79
CAESAR   Till which encounter,
  It is my business too. Farewell.
LEPIDUS
  Farewell, my lord. What you shall know meantime
  Of stirs abroad, I shall beseech you, sir,
  To let me be partaker.
CAESAR   Doubt not, sir ;
  I knew it for my bond.   *Exeunt.* 84

*

62 *stale* urine; *gilded* yellow-colored   71 *lanked* thinned   78 *be able* muster   79 *front* cope with   84 *bond* duty

I, v   *Enter Cleopatra, Charmian, Iras, and Mardian.*

CLEOPATRA Charmian!

CHARMIAN Madam?

CLEOPATRA

3   Ha, ha.

4   Give me to drink mandragora.

CHARMIAN   Why, madam?

CLEOPATRA

That I might sleep out this great gap of time

My Antony is away.

CHARMIAN   You think of him too much.

CLEOPATRA

O, 'tis treason!

CHARMIAN   Madam, I trust, not so.

CLEOPATRA

Thou, eunuch Mardian!

MARDIAN   What's your Highness' pleasure?

CLEOPATRA

Not now to hear thee sing. I take no pleasure

In aught an eunuch has: 'tis well for thee

11   That, being unseminared, thy freer thoughts

May not fly forth of Egypt. Hast thou affections?

MARDIAN Yes, gracious madam.

CLEOPATRA Indeed?

MARDIAN

Not in deed, madam; for I can do nothing

But what indeed is honest to be done:

Yet have I fierce affections, and think

What Venus did with Mars.

CLEOPATRA   O Charmian,

Where think'st thou he is now? Stands he, or sits he?

Or does he walk? or is he on his horse?

O happy horse, to bear the weight of Antony!

22   Do bravely, horse! for wot'st thou whom thou mov'st?

I, v The chambers of Cleopatra 3 *Ha, ha* (perhaps indicating a yawn)
4 *mandragora* mandrake (a narcotic) 11 *unseminared* unsexed 22 *wot'st* knowest

The demi-Atlas of this earth, the arm   23
And burgonet of men. He's speaking now,   24
Or murmuring, 'Where's my serpent of old Nile?'
(For so he calls me). Now I feed myself
With most delicious poison. Think on me,
That am with Phoebus' amorous pinches black   28
And wrinkled deep in time? Broad-fronted Caesar,   29
When thou wast here above the ground, I was
A morsel for a monarch; and great Pompey
Would stand and make his eyes grow in my brow;
There would he anchor his aspect, and die   33
With looking on his life.
     Enter Alexas.
ALEXAS   Sovereign of Egypt, hail!
CLEOPATRA
How much unlike art thou Mark Antony!
Yet, coming from him, that great med'cine hath   36
With his tinct gilded thee.
How goes it with my brave Mark Antony?   38
ALEXAS
Last thing he did, dear Queen,
He kissed – the last of many doubled kisses –
This orient pearl. His speech sticks in my heart.   41
CLEOPATRA
Mine ear must pluck it thence.
ALEXAS   'Good friend,' quoth he,
'Say the firm Roman to great Egypt sends   43
This treasure of an oyster; at whose foot,
To mend the petty present, I will piece
Her opulent throne with kingdoms. All the East
(Say thou) shall call her mistress.' So he nodded,

---

23 *demi-Atlas* i.e. Antony and Caesar, like Atlas, support the world between them (Lepidus being of no importance)   **24** *burgonet* helmet   **28** *Phoebus'* the sun's   **29** *Broad-fronted* with broad forehead; *Caesar* Julius Caesar   **33** *aspect* gaze   **36–37** *that . . . thee* (Cleopatra playfully compares Antony to the 'great medicine' of the alchemists which turned baser metals to gold: even Alexas shows some effect)   **38** *brave* splendid   **41** *orient* i.e. bright as the east   **43** *firm* constant

48   And soberly did mount an arm-gaunt steed,
       Who neighed so high that what I would have spoke
50   Was beastly dumbed by him.

CLEOPATRA   What was he, sad or merry?

ALEXAS
       Like to the time o' th' year between the extremes
       Of hot and cold, he was nor sad nor merry.

CLEOPATRA
       O well-divided disposition! Note him,
54   Note him, good Charmian, 'tis the man; but note him.
       He was not sad, for he would shine on those
       That make their looks by his; he was not merry,
       Which seemed to tell them his remembrance lay
       In Egypt with his joy; but between both.
       O heavenly mingle! Be'st thou sad or merry,
       The violence of either thee becomes,
61   So does it no man else. – Met'st thou my posts?

ALEXAS
       Ay, madam, twenty several messengers.
       Why do you send so thick?

CLEOPATRA   Who's born that day
       When I forget to send to Antony
       Shall die a beggar. Ink and paper, Charmian.
       Welcome, my good Alexas. Did I, Charmian,
       Ever love Caesar so?

CHARMIAN   O that brave Caesar!

CLEOPATRA
       Be choked with such another emphasis!
       Say 'the brave Antony.'

CHARMIAN   The valiant Caesar!

CLEOPATRA
       By Isis, I will give thee bloody teeth
71   If thou with Caesar paragon again
       My man of men.

---

48 *arm-gaunt* toughened for war (?), battle-hungry (?)   50 *dumbed*
silenced   54 *the man* i.e. the real Antony   61 *posts* messengers   71 *paragon*
compare

CHARMIAN   By your most gracious pardon,
  I sing but after you.
CLEOPATRA   My salad days,   73
  When I was green in judgment, cold in blood,   *> seemingly
  To say as I said then. But come, away,   contradictory
  Get me ink and paper.   of green, youth
  He shall have every day a several greeting,
  Or I'll unpeople Egypt.   *Exeunt.* 78

                        *

      Enter Pompey, Menecrates, and Menas, in warlike   II, i
      manner.
POMPEY
  If the great gods be just, they shall assist
  The deeds of justest men.
MENECRATES   Know, worthy Pompey,
  That what they do delay, they not deny.
POMPEY
  Whiles we are suitors to their throne, decays   4
  The thing we sue for.
MENECRATES   We, ignorant of ourselves,
  Beg often our own harms, which the wise pow'rs
  Deny us for our good : so find we profit
  By losing of our prayers.
POMPEY   I shall do well :
  The people love me, and the sea is mine ;
  My powers are crescent, and my auguring hope   10
  Says it will come to th' full. Mark Antony   11
  In Egypt sits at dinner, and will make
  No wars without doors. Caesar gets money where
  He loses hearts. Lepidus flatters both,
  Of both is flattered ; but he neither loves,
  Nor either cares for him.

73 *salad days* green youth   78 *unpeople* i.e. by sending messengers to
Antony
II, i Pompey's house in Messina   4–5 *Whiles . . . for* i.e. the thing we pray
for loses its worth even while we pray   10 *crescent* increasing   11 *it* i.e.
my fortunes (imaged as a crescent moon)

MENAS   Caesar and Lepidus
Are in the field ; a mighty strength they carry.

POMPEY
Where have you this ? 'Tis false.

MENAS   From Silvius, sir.

POMPEY
He dreams : I know they are in Rome together,
Looking for Antony. But all the charms of love,
21   Salt Cleopatra, soften thy waned lip !
Let witchcraft join with beauty, lust with both !
Tie up the libertine in a field of feasts,
Keep his brain fuming. Epicurean cooks
25   Sharpen with cloyless sauce his appetite,
26   That sleep and feeding may prorogue his honor
27   Even till a Lethe'd dulness –
                Enter Varrius.   How now, Varrius ?

VARRIUS
This is most certain that I shall deliver :
Mark Antony is every hour in Rome
Expected. Since he went from Egypt 'tis
31   A space for farther travel.

POMPEY   I could have given less matter
A better ear. Menas, I did not think
33   This amorous surfeiter would have donned his helm
For such a petty war. His soldiership
Is twice the other twain. But let us rear
36   The higher our opinion, that our stirring
Can from the lap of Egypt's widow pluck
The ne'er-lust-wearied Antony.

38 MENAS   I cannot hope
39   Caesar and Antony shall well greet together ;
His wife that's dead did trespasses to Caesar ;

---

21 *Salt* lustful; *waned* faded   25 *cloyless* which never cloys   26 *prorogue*
suspend   27 *Lethe'd dulness* i.e. an oblivion as deep as that which comes
from drinking of the river Lethe in the underworld   31 *A space . . . travel*
time enough for even a longer journey   33 *surfeiter* one who indulges to
excess   36 *opinion* i.e. of ourselves   38 *hope* expect   39 *greet* get on

His brother warred upon him; although I think   41
Not moved by Antony.
POMPEY   I know not, Menas,
How lesser enmities may give way to greater.
Were't not that we stand up against them all,
'Twere pregnant they should square between them-   45
    selves,
For they have entertainèd cause enough
To draw their swords; but how the fear of us
May cement their divisions and bind up
The petty difference, we yet not know.
Be't as our gods will have't! It only stands   50
Our lives upon to use our strongest hands.
Come, Menas.   *Exeunt.*

*

Enter Enobarbus and Lepidus.   II, ii
LEPIDUS
Good Enobarbus, 'tis a worthy deed,
And shall become you well, to entreat your captain
To soft and gentle speech.
ENOBARBUS   I shall entreat him
To answer like himself: if Caesar move him,   4
Let Antony look over Caesar's head
And speak as loud as Mars. By Jupiter,
Were I the wearer of Antonio's beard,
I would not shave't to-day!   8
LEPIDUS   'Tis not a time
For private stomaching.   9
ENOBARBUS   Every time
Serves for the matter that is then born in't.
LEPIDUS
But small to greater matters must give way.

---

41 *brother* (cf. I, ii, 84–90) 45 *pregnant* likely; *square* quarrel 50–51
stands . . . upon is a matter of life and death
II, ii The house of Lepidus in Rome 4 *like himself* as befits his greatness
8 *I . . . shave't* i.e. I would dare Caesar to pluck it 9 *stomaching* resentment

ENOBARBUS
    Not if the small come first.
LEPIDUS   Your speech is passion;
    But pray you stir no embers up. Here comes
    The noble Antony.
            Enter Antony and Ventidius.
ENOBARBUS   And yonder, Caesar.
            Enter Caesar, Maecenas, and Agrippa.
ANTONY
15 If we compose well here, to Parthia.
    Hark, Ventidius.
CAESAR   I do not know,
    Maecenas; ask Agrippa.
LEPIDUS   Noble friends,
    That which combined us was most great, and let not
    A leaner action rend us. What's amiss,
    May it be gently heard. When we debate
    Our trivial difference loud, we do commit
    Murder in healing wounds. Then, noble partners,
23 The rather for I earnestly beseech,
    Touch you the sourest points with sweetest terms,
25 Nor curstness grow to th' matter.
ANTONY   'Tis spoken well.
    Were we before our armies, and to fight,
27 I should do thus.
            Flourish.
CAESAR
    Welcome to Rome.
ANTONY   Thank you.
CAESAR   Sit.
ANTONY   Sit, sir.
CAESAR   Nay then.
        [They sit.]

15 *compose* reach agreement   23 *The rather for* all the more because   25
Nor ... matter and let not ill temper make matters worse   27 *thus* (Antony
makes some courteous gesture)

ANTONY
    I learn you take things ill which are not so,
    Or being, concern you not.

CAESAR   I must be laughed at
    If, or for nothing or a little, I   31
    Should say myself offended, and with you
    Chiefly i' th' world; more laughed at that I should
    Once name you derogately, when to sound your name   34
    It not concerned me.

ANTONY   My being in Egypt, Caesar,
    What was't to you?

CAESAR
    No more than my residing here at Rome
    Might be to you in Egypt: yet if you there
    Did practice on my state, your being in Egypt   39
    Might be my question.   40

ANTONY   How intend you? practiced?

CAESAR
    You may be pleased to catch at mine intent
    By what did here befall me. Your wife and brother
    Made wars upon me, and their contestation
    Was theme for you; you were the word of war.   44

ANTONY
    You do mistake your business: my brother never
    Did urge me in his act. I did inquire it   46
    And have my learning from some true reports   47
    That drew their swords with you. Did he not rather
    Discredit my authority with yours,
    And make the wars alike against my stomach,   50
    Having alike your cause? Of this my letters   51
    Before did satisfy you. If you'll patch a quarrel,   52

---

31 *or . . . or* either . . . or   34 *derogately* disparagingly   39 *practice on* plot
against   40 *question* concern   44 *you were . . . war* the war was carried on in
your name   46 *urge me* use my name   47 *reports* reporters   50 *stomach*
desire   51 *Having . . . cause* i.e. I having as much cause as you to resent it
52–54 *If . . . this* i.e. if you are determined to patch a quarrel out of pieces,
when you actually have whole cloth to fashion it from (cf. ll. 81–98), this
is not the right piece

As matter whole you have to make it with,
It must not be with this.

CAESAR   You praise yourself
By laying defects of judgment to me, but
You patched up your excuses.

ANTONY   Not so, not so:
I know you could not lack, I am certain on't,
Very necessity of this thought, that I,
Your partner in the cause 'gainst which he fought,
60   Could not with graceful eyes attend those wars
Which fronted mine own peace. As for my wife,
I would you had her spirit in such another;
63   The third o' th' world is yours, which with a snaffle
64   You may pace easy, but not such a wife.

ENOBARBUS Would we had all such wives, that the men
might go to wars with the women.

ANTONY
67   So much uncurbable, her garboils, Caesar,
Made out of her impatience – which not wanted
Shrewdness of policy too – I grieving grant
Did you too much disquiet: for that you must
But say I could not help it.

CAESAR   I wrote to you
When rioting in Alexandria; you
Did pocket up my letters, and with taunts
74   Did gibe my missive out of audience.

ANTONY   Sir,
He fell upon me, ere admitted, then:
76   Three kings I had newly feasted, and did want
Of what I was i' th' morning; but next day
78   I told him of myself, which was as much
As to have asked him pardon. Let this fellow
Be nothing of our strife: if we contend,
81   Out of our question wipe him.

60 *with . . . attend* regard with pleasure 63 *snaffle* bridle bit 64 *pace* manage 67 *garboils* commotions 74 *missive* messenger 76–77 *did . . . morning* was not myself 78 *myself* my condition 81 *question* argument

54

CAESAR   You have broken
  The article of your oath, which you shall never
  Have tongue to charge me with.
LEPIDUS   Soft, Caesar.
ANTONY   No,
  Lepidus; let him speak.
  The honor is sacred which he talks on now,   85
  Supposing that I lacked it. But on, Caesar,
  The article of my oath –
CAESAR
  To lend me arms and aid when I required them,
  The which you both denied.
ANTONY   Neglected rather:
  And then when poisonèd hours had bound me up   90
  From mine own knowledge. As nearly as I may,
  I'll play the penitent to you. But mine honesty   92
  Shall not make poor my greatness, nor my power
  Work without it. Truth is, that Fulvia,
  To have me out of Egypt, made wars here,
  For which myself, the ignorant motive, do
  So far ask pardon as befits mine honor
  To stoop in such a case.
LEPIDUS   'Tis noble spoken.
MAECENAS
  If it might please you, to enforce no further
  The griefs between ye: to forget them quite
  Were to remember that the present need
  Speaks to atone you.   102
LEPIDUS   Worthily spoken, Maecenas.
ENOBARBUS Or, if you borrow one another's love for the
  instant, you may, when you hear no more words of
  Pompey, return it again: you shall have time to wrangle
  in when you have nothing else to do.

85 *honor* i.e. keeping an oath   90–91 *bound . . . knowledge* i.e. prevented my
realizing what I was doing   92–94 *mine . . . it* i.e. my actions will be
prompted by my honesty (which makes me willing to apologize) but also
by my power (which does not intend to grovel)   102 *atone* reconcile

55

ANTONY
Thou art a soldier only, speak no more.

ENOBARBUS That truth should be silent I had almost
forgot.

ANTONY

109 You wrong this presence, therefore speak no more.

110 ENOBARBUS Go to, then; your considerate stone.

CAESAR
I do not much dislike the matter, but
The manner of his speech; for't cannot be
We shall remain in friendship, our conditions
So diff'ring in their acts. Yet if I knew
What hoop should hold us staunch, from edge to edge
O' th' world I would pursue it.

AGRIPPA   Give me leave, Caesar.

CAESAR
Speak, Agrippa.

AGRIPPA
Thou hast a sister by the mother's side,
Admired Octavia: great Mark Antony
Is now a widower.

CAESAR   Say not so, Agrippa:
If Cleopatra heard you, your reproof

122 Were well deserved of rashness.

ANTONY
I am not married, Caesar: let me hear
Agrippa further speak.

AGRIPPA
To hold you in perpetual amity,
To make you brothers, and to knit your hearts
With an unslipping knot, take Antony
Octavia to his wife; whose beauty claims
No worse a husband than the best of men;

---

109 *presence* company **110** *your considerate stone* i.e. I'll be dumb as a stone,
but still thinking (considering) **122** *of rashness* because of your rashness
(in ignoring Antony's bond to Cleopatra)

Whose virtue and whose general graces speak
That which none else can utter. By this marriage
All little jealousies, which now seem great,   132
And all great fears, which now import their dangers,
Would then be nothing : truths would be tales,   134
Where now half-tales be truths : her love to both
Would each to other, and all loves to both,
Draw after her. Pardon what I have spoke ;
For 'tis a studied, not a present thought,
By duty ruminated.

ANTONY   Will Caesar speak ?

CAESAR

Not till he hears how Antony is touched
With what is spoke already.

ANTONY   What power is in Agrippa,
If I would say, 'Agrippa, be it so,'
To make this good ?

CAESAR   The power of Caesar, and
His power unto Octavia.

ANTONY   May I never
To this good purpose, that so fairly shows,   145
Dream of impediment : let me have thy hand :
Further this act of grace, and from this hour   147
The heart of brothers govern in our loves
And sway our great designs.

CAESAR   There's my hand.
A sister I bequeath you, whom no brother
Did ever love so dearly. Let her live
To join our kingdoms and our hearts ; and never   152
Fly off our loves again.

LEPIDUS   Happily, amen.

ANTONY

I did not think to draw my sword 'gainst Pompey,

---

132 *jealousies* misunderstandings   134–35 *would be . . . be* would be taken
for . . . are taken for   145 *so fairly shows* looks so hopeful   147 *grace*
reconciliation   152–53 *never . . . loves* never may we be estranged

155 For he hath laid strange courtesies and great
Of late upon me. I must thank him only,
157 Lest my remembrance suffer ill report:
At heel of that, defy him.
LEPIDUS   Time calls upon's.
159 Of us must Pompey presently be sought,
Or else he seeks out us.
ANTONY   Where lies he?
CAESAR
161 About the Mount Mesena.
ANTONY
What is his strength by land?
CAESAR
Great and increasing; but by sea
He is an absolute master.
164 ANTONY   So is the fame.
Would we had spoke together! Haste we for it,
Yet, ere we put ourselves in arms, dispatch we
The business we have talked of.
CAESAR   With most gladness;
And do invite you to my sister's view,
Whither straight I'll lead you.
ANTONY   Let us, Lepidus,
Not lack your company.
LEPIDUS   Noble Antony,
Not sickness should detain me.   *Flourish. [Exeunt.]*
                    Mane[n]t Enobarbus, Agrippa, Maecenas.
MAECENAS Welcome from Egypt, sir.
173 ENOBARBUS Half the heart of Caesar, worthy Maecenas.
My honorable friend, Agrippa.
AGRIPPA Good Enobarbus.
MAECENAS We have cause to be glad that matters are so
177 well disgested. You stayed well by't in Egypt.

---

155 *strange* unusual   157 *remembrance* readiness to acknowledge favors
159 *presently* at once   161 *Mesena* i.e. Misenum, an Italian port   164
fame report   173 *Half* i.e. sharing it with Agrippa   177 *disgested* digested,
arranged; *stayed . . . by't* kept at it, 'lived it up'

ENOBARBUS Ay, sir, we did sleep day out of countenance 178
and made the night light with drinking.

MAECENAS Eight wild boars roasted whole at a breakfast,
and but twelve persons there. Is this true?

ENOBARBUS This was but as a fly by an eagle: we had 182
much more monstrous matter of feast, which worthily
deserved noting.

MAECENAS She's a most triumphant lady, if report be
square to her.   186

ENOBARBUS When she first met Mark Antony, she pursed 187
up his heart, upon the river of Cydnus.

AGRIPPA There she appeared indeed; or my reporter de- 189
vised well for her.

ENOBARBUS
I will tell you.
The barge she sat in, like a burnished throne,
Burned on the water: the poop was beaten gold;
Purple the sails, and so perfumèd that
The winds were lovesick with them; the oars were silver,
Which to the tune of flutes kept stroke, and made
The water which they beat to follow faster,
As amorous of their strokes. For her own person,
It beggared all description: she did lie
In her pavilion, cloth-of-gold of tissue,   200
O'erpicturing that Venus where we see   201
The fancy outwork nature. On each side her   202
Stood pretty dimpled boys, like smiling Cupids,
With divers-colored fans, whose wind did seem
To glow the delicate cheeks which they did cool,   205
And what they undid did.

178–79 *we . . . drinking* i.e. we ruffled the dignity of day (personified) by
sleeping through it, and made night light (i.e. bright, lightheaded, and
wanton) with drinking parties 182 *by* compared to 186 *square* fair
187–88 *pursed up* pocketed (but with a suggestion of pursed lips for kissing)
189 *appeared* came before the public; *devised* invented 200 *cloth-of-gold
of tissue* cloth interwoven with gold threads 201 *O'erpicturing* outdoing
the picture of 202 *fancy* i.e. the painter's imagination 205 *glow* make
glow (as if heated)

AGRIPPA   O, rare for Antony.

ENOBARBUS

207   Her gentlewomen, like the Nereides,
208   So many mermaids, tended her i' th' eyes,
209   And made their bends adornings. At the helm
       A seeming mermaid steers: the silken tackle
       Swell with the touches of those flower-soft hands,
212   That yarely frame the office. From the barge
       A strange invisible perfume hits the sense
       Of the adjacent wharfs. The city cast
       Her people out upon her; and Antony,
       Enthroned i' th' market place, did sit alone,
217   Whistling to th' air; which, but for vacancy,
       Had gone to gaze on Cleopatra too,
       And made a gap in nature.

AGRIPPA   Rare Egyptian!

ENOBARBUS

       Upon her landing, Antony sent to her,
       Invited her to supper. She replied,
       It should be better he became her guest;
       Which she entreated. Our courteous Antony,
       Whom ne'er the word of 'no' woman heard speak,
       Being barbered ten times o'er, goes to the feast,
226   And for his ordinary pays his heart
       For what his eyes eat only.

AGRIPPA   Royal wench!

       She made great Caesar lay his sword to bed;
229   He ploughed her, and she cropped.

ENOBARBUS   I saw her once

       Hop forty paces through the public street;
       And having lost her breath, she spoke, and panted,

---

207 *Nereides* sea nymphs   208 *tended . . . eyes* waited on her every glance
209 *made . . . adornings* made their postures of submission decorative
(as in a tableau)   212 *yarely frame* nimbly perform   217 *but for vacancy*
except that it would have left a vacuum   226 *ordinary* meal   229 *cropped*
bore fruit (i.e. Julius Caesar's son, Caesarion)

II, ii

That she did make defect perfection   232
And, breathless, pow'r breathe forth.

MAECENAS
Now Antony must leave her utterly.

ENOBARBUS
Never; he will not:
Age cannot wither her, nor custom stale
Her infinite variety: other women cloy
The appetites they feed, but she makes hungry
Where most she satisfies. For vilest things
Become themselves in her, that the holy priests   240
Bless her when she is riggish.   241

MAECENAS
If beauty, wisdom, modesty, can settle
The heart of Antony, Octavia is
A blessèd lottery to him.   244

AGRIPPA   Let us go.
Good Enobarbus, make yourself my guest
Whilst you abide here.

ENOBARBUS   Humbly, sir, I thank you. *Exeunt.*

*

Enter Antony, Caesar, Octavia between them.   **II, iii**

ANTONY
The world and my great office will sometimes
Divide me from your bosom.

OCTAVIA   All which time
Before the gods my knee shall bow my prayers
To them for you.

ANTONY   Good night, sir. My Octavia,
Read not my blemishes in the world's report:
I have not kept my square, but that to come   6

---

232 *defect* i.e. the resulting breathlessness **240** *Become . . . her* are so
becoming to her **241** *riggish* lewd **244** *lottery* gift of fortune
II, iii The house of Octavius Caesar **6** *square* carpenter's square (i.e. I
have not followed the straight and narrow)

> Shall all be done by th' rule. Good night, dear lady.

OCTAVIA Good night, sir.

CAESAR Good night.   *Exit [with Octavia].*
            Enter Soothsayer.

ANTONY

> Now, sirrah : you do wish yourself in Egypt ?

SOOTHSAYER

> Would I had never come from thence, nor you thither.

ANTONY

> If you can, your reason ?

SOOTHSAYER

14 I see it in my motion, have it not in my tongue,
    But yet hie you to Egypt again.

ANTONY   Say to me,
    Whose fortunes shall rise higher, Caesar's or mine ?

SOOTHSAYER Caesar's.
    Therefore, O Antony, stay not by his side.

19 Thy demon, that thy spirit which keeps thee, is
    Noble, courageous, high, unmatchable,
    Where Caesar's is not. But near him thy angel

22 Becomes a fear, as being o'erpow'red. Therefore
    Make space enough between you.

ANTONY   Speak this no more.

SOOTHSAYER

> To none but thee, no more but when to thee.
> If thou dost play with him at any game,
> Thou art sure to lose ; and of that natural luck

27 He beats thee 'gainst the odds. Thy lustre thickens
    When he shines by : I say again, thy spirit
    Is all afraid to govern thee near him ;
    But he away, 'tis noble.

ANTONY   Get thee gone.
    Say to Ventidius I would speak with him.

                              Exit [Soothsayer].

---

14 *motion* mind   19 *demon* guardian angel   22 *a fear* i.e. timorous   27
thickens dims

He shall to Parthia. – Be it art or hap,   32
He hath spoken true. The very dice obey him,
And in our sports my better cunning faints   34
Under his chance : if we draw lots, he speeds ;   35
His cocks do win the battle still of mine   36
When it is all to naught, and his quails ever   37
Beat mine, inhooped, at odds. I will to Egypt :   38
And though I make this marriage for my peace,
I' th' East my pleasure lies.
    Enter Ventidius.   O, come, Ventidius,
You must to Parthia. Your commission 's ready :
Follow me, and receive't.   *Exeunt.*

*

Enter Lepidus, Maecenas, and Agrippa.   II, iv

LEPIDUS Trouble yourselves no further : pray you, hasten your generals after.

AGRIPPA Sir, Mark Antony will e'en but kiss Octavia, and we'll follow.

LEPIDUS Till I shall see you in your soldier's dress, which will become you both, farewell.

MAECENAS We shall, as I conceive the journey, be at Mount before you, Lepidus.   8

LEPIDUS Your way is shorter ; my purposes do draw me much about : you'll win two days upon me.   10

BOTH Sir, good success.

LEPIDUS Farewell.   *Exeunt.*

*

32 *art or hap* skill or chance   34 *cunning* skill   35 *chance* luck; *speeds* wins
36 *still* always   37 *it . . . naught* i.e. the odds are everything to nothing in
my favor   38 *inhooped* i.e. fighting confined within a hoop
II, iv Before the house of Lepidus   8 *Mount* (cf. II, ii, 161)   10 *about*
roundabout

II, v   *Enter Cleopatra, Charmian, Iras, and Alexas.*

CLEOPATRA
Give me some music: music, moody food
Of us that trade in love.

OMNES   The music, ho!
Enter Mardian the Eunuch.

CLEOPATRA
Let it alone, let's to billiards: come, Charmian.

CHARMIAN
My arm is sore; best play with Mardian.

CLEOPATRA
As well a woman with an eunuch played
As with a woman. Come, you'll play with me, sir?

MARDIAN As well as I can, madam.

CLEOPATRA
And when good will is showed, though't come too short,
The actor may plead pardon. I'll none now.
10   Give me mine angle, we'll to th' river: there,
My music playing far off, I will betray
Tawny-finned fishes. My bended hook shall pierce
Their slimy jaws; and as I draw them up,
I'll think them every one an Antony,
And say, 'Ah, ha! y' are caught!'

CHARMIAN   'Twas merry when
You wagered on your angling, when your diver
17   Did hang a salt fish on his hook, which he
With fervency drew up.

CLEOPATRA   That time – O times! –
I laughed him out of patience; and that night
I laughed him into patience; and next morn
Ere the ninth hour I drunk him to his bed;
22   Then put my tires and mantles on him, whilst
23   I wore his sword Philippan.
          Enter a Messenger.   O, from Italy!

II, v The chambers of Cleopatra in her palace at Alexandria   10 *angle*
fishing tackle 17 *salt* dried 22 *tires* headdresses 23 *Philippan* (so
called because he had beaten Brutus and Cassius with it at Philippi)

Ram thou thy fruitful tidings in mine ears,
That long time have been barren.
MESSENGER   Madam, madam –
CLEOPATRA
  Antonio's dead : if thou say so, villain,
  Thou kill'st thy mistress : but well and free,
  If thou so yield him, there is gold and here
  My bluest veins to kiss, a hand that kings
  Have lipped, and trembled kissing.
MESSENGER
  First, madam, he is well.
CLEOPATRA   Why, there's more gold.
  But, sirrah, mark, we use
  To say the dead are well : bring it to that,   33
  The gold I give thee will I melt and pour
  Down thy ill-uttering throat.
MESSENGER
  Good madam, hear me.
CLEOPATRA   Well, go to, I will :
  But there's no goodness in thy face if Antony   37
  Be free and healthful ; so tart a favor   38
  To trumpet such good tidings ? If not well,
  Thou shouldst come like a Fury crowned with snakes,
  Not like a formal man.   41
MESSENGER   Will't please you hear me ?
CLEOPATRA
  I have a mind to strike thee ere thou speak'st :
  Yet, if thou say Antony lives, is well,
  Or friends with Caesar, or not captive to him,
  I'll set thee in a shower of gold, and hail
  Rich pearls upon thee.
MESSENGER   Madam, he's well.
CLEOPATRA   Well said.
MESSENGER
  And friends with Caesar.

33 *well* i.e. in heaven; *bring . . . that* say that you mean that   37 *goodness*
i.e. truth   38 *tart a favor* sour a face   41 *Not . . . man* not in human shape

CLEOPATRA   Th' art an honest man.

MESSENGER
Caesar and he are greater friends than ever.

CLEOPATRA
Make thee a fortune from me.

MESSENGER   But yet, madam –

CLEOPATRA
50   I do not like 'but yet,' it does allay
The good precedence : fie upon 'but yet,'
'But yet' is as a jailer to bring forth
Some monstrous malefactor. Prithee, friend,
Pour out the pack of matter to mine ear,
The good and bad together : he's friends with Caesar,
In state of health, thou say'st, and thou say'st, free.

MESSENGER
Free, madam, no : I made no such report,
He's bound unto Octavia.

CLEOPATRA   For what good turn ?

MESSENGER
For the best turn i' th' bed.

CLEOPATRA   I am pale, Charmian.

MESSENGER
Madam, he's married to Octavia.

CLEOPATRA
The most infectious pestilence upon thee !
    Strikes him down.

MESSENGER
Good madam, patience.

CLEOPATRA   What say you ?
    Strikes him.   Hence,
63   Horrible villain ! or I'll spurn thine eyes
64   Like balls before me : I'll unhair thy head,
    She hales him up and down.
Thou shalt be whipped with wire and stewed in brine,
66   Smarting in ling'ring pickle.

50–51 *allay . . . precedence* spoil the good that preceded it   63 *spurn* kick
64 s.d. *hales* drags 66 *pickle* pickling solution

MESSENGER   Gracious madam,
I that do bring the news made not the match.
CLEOPATRA
Say 'tis not so, a province I will give thee,
And make thy fortunes proud : the blow thou hadst
Shall make thy peace for moving me to rage,
And I will boot thee with what gift beside   71
Thy modesty can beg.   72
MESSENGER   He's married, madam.
CLEOPATRA
Rogue, thou hast lived too long.
            Draw a knife.
MESSENGER   Nay, then I'll run.
What mean you, madam ? I have made no fault.   *Exit.*
CHARMIAN
Good madam, keep yourself within yourself,
The man is innocent.
CLEOPATRA
Some innocents 'scape not the thunderbolt.
Melt Egypt into Nile ! and kindly creatures
Turn all to serpents ! Call the slave again :
Though I am mad, I will not bite him. Call !
CHARMIAN
He is afeard to come.
CLEOPATRA   I will not hurt him. *[Exit Charmian.]*
These hands do lack nobility, that they strike
A meaner than myself ; since I myself
Have given myself the cause.   84
            Enter [Charmian and] the Messenger again.
                              Come hither, sir.
Though it be honest, it is never good
To bring bad news : give to a gracious message
An host of tongues, but let ill tidings tell
Themselves when they be felt.
MESSENGER   I have done my duty.

71 *boot* benefit   72 *modesty* humble condition   84 *cause* i.e. by loving
Antony

CLEOPATRA
Is he married?
I cannot hate thee worser than I do
If thou again say 'Yes.'

MESSENGER   He's married, madam.

CLEOPATRA
92   The gods confound thee! Dost thou hold there still?

MESSENGER
Should I lie, madam?

CLEOPATRA   O, I would thou didst,
94   So half my Egypt were submerged and made
A cistern for scaled snakes! Go get thee hence;
96   Hadst thou Narcissus in thy face, to me
Thou wouldst appear most ugly. He is married?

MESSENGER
I crave your Highness' pardon.

CLEOPATRA   He is married?

MESSENGER
99   Take no offense that I would not offend you:
To punish me for what you make me do
101 Seems much unequal: he's married to Octavia.

CLEOPATRA
O, that his fault should make a knave of thee,
103 That art not what th' art sure of! Get thee hence,
The merchandise which thou hast brought from Rome
105 Are all too dear for me. Lie they upon thy hand,
106 And be undone by 'em!   [Exit Messenger.]

CHARMIAN   Good your Highness, patience.

CLEOPATRA
In praising Antony I have dispraised Caesar.

CHARMIAN
Many times, madam.

92 *confound* destroy   94 *So* even though   96 *Hadst . . . face* were you as
handsome as Narcissus (in Greek legend, the youth who fell in love with his
image reflected in a stream)   99 *Take . . . you* don't be angry that I'd
rather not anger you (i.e. by answering)   101 *unequal* unjust   103 *That . . .
of* i.e. who are not really hateful, like the news you bring   105 *upon thy
hand* i.e. unsold   106 *undone* bankrupt

CLEOPATRA   I am paid for't now.
Lead me from hence,
I faint. O Iras, Charmian ! 'Tis no matter.
Go to the fellow, good Alexas ; bid him
Report the feature of Octavia : her years,
Her inclination, let him not leave out
The color of her hair. Bring me word quickly.
                        [Exit Alexas.]
Let him for ever go ! – let him not ! – Charmian,
Though he be painted one way like a Gorgon,   116
The other way 's a Mars. *[to Mardian]* Bid you Alexas
Bring me word how tall she is. – Pity me, Charmian,
But do not speak to me. Lead me to my chamber.
                              Exeunt.

✳

Flourish. Enter Pompey at one door, with Drum and II, vi
Trumpet : at another, Caesar, Lepidus, Antony,
Enobarbus, Maecenas, Agrippa, Menas, with
Soldiers marching.

POMPEY
Your hostages I have, so have you mine ;
And we shall talk before we fight.
CAESAR   Most meet   2
That first we come to words, and therefore have we
Our written purposes before us sent ;
Which if thou hast considerèd, let us know
If 'twill tie up thy discontented sword
And carry back to Sicily much tall youth   7
That else must perish here.
POMPEY   To you all three,
The senators alone of this great world,
Chief factors for the gods : I do not know   10
Wherefore my father should revengers want,

116 *Gorgon* Medusa (the sight of whose ugly face turned men to stone)
II, vi An open place near Misenum **2** *meet* suitable **7** *tall* bold **10**
factors agents

Having a son and friends, since Julius Caesar,
13 Who at Philippi the good Brutus ghosted,
There saw you laboring for him. What was't
That moved pale Cassius to conspire? And what
Made all-honored, honest, Roman Brutus,
With the armed rest, courtiers of beauteous freedom,
To drench the Capitol, but that they would
Have one man but a man? And that is it
Hath made me rig my navy, at whose burden
The angered ocean foams; with which I meant
To scourge th' ingratitude that despiteful Rome
Cast on my noble father.

CAESAR   Take your time.

ANTONY
24 Thou canst not fear us, Pompey, with thy sails.
25 We'll speak with thee at sea. At land thou know'st
26 How much we do o'ercount thee.

POMPEY   At land indeed
27 Thou dost o'ercount me of my father's house:
28 But since the cuckoo builds not for himself,
29 Remain in't as thou mayst.

LEPIDUS   Be pleased to tell us
30 (For this is from the present) how you take
The offers we have sent you.

CAESAR   There's the point.

ANTONY
Which do not be entreated to, but weigh
33 What it is worth embraced.

CAESAR   And what may follow,
34 To try a larger fortune.

POMPEY   You have made me offer
Of Sicily, Sardinia; and I must

---

13 *ghosted* haunted   24 *fear* frighten   25 *speak* contest   26 *o'ercount* outnumber   27 *o'ercount* cheat; *house* (Plutarch says that Antony had bought this house but not paid for it)   28 *cuckoo* (which never builds its own nest but lays its eggs in the nests of other birds)   29 *as thou mayst* as long as you can   30 *from the present* off the topic   33 *embraced* if accepted   34 *a larger fortune* i.e. war with the triumvirs

Rid all the sea of pirates ; then, to send
Measures of wheat to Rome ; this 'greed upon,
To part with unhacked edges and bear back   38
Our targes undinted.   39

OMNES   That's our offer.

POMPEY   Know then
I came before you here a man prepared
To take this offer ; but Mark Antony
Put me to some impatience. Though I lose
The praise of it by telling, you must know,
When Caesar and your brother were at blows,
Your mother came to Sicily and did find
Her welcome friendly.

ANTONY   I have heard it, Pompey,
And am well studied for a liberal thanks,   47
Which I do owe you.

POMPEY   Let me have your hand :
I did not think, sir, to have met you here.

ANTONY
The beds i' th' East are soft ; and thanks to you,
That called me timelier than my purpose hither ;
For I have gained by't.

CAESAR   Since I saw you last
There's a change upon you.

POMPEY   Well, I know not
What counts harsh fortune casts upon my face,   54
But in my bosom shall she never come
To make my heart her vassal.

LEPIDUS   Well met here.

POMPEY
I hope so, Lepidus. Thus we are agreed.
I crave our composition may be written,   58
And sealed between us.

CAESAR   That's the next to do.

38 *edges* swords   39 *targes* shields; *Omnes* all (Antony, Caesar, Lepidus)
47 *studied for* prepared with   54 *counts* tallies (as on a scoring stick)   58
composition agreement

POMPEY
　We'll feast each other ere we part, and let's
　Draw lots who shall begin.

ANTONY   That will I, Pompey.

POMPEY
　No, Antony, take the lot:
　But, first or last, your fine Egyptian cookery
　Shall have the fame. I have heard that Julius Caesar
　Grew fat with feasting there.

ANTONY   You have heard much.

POMPEY
　I have fair meanings, sir.

ANTONY   And fair words to them.

POMPEY
　Then so much have I heard,
　And I have heard Apollodorus carried –

ENOBARBUS
　No more of that: he did so.

POMPEY   What, I pray you?

ENOBARBUS
　A certain queen to Caesar in a mattress.

POMPEY
　I know thee now; how far'st thou, soldier?

ENOBARBUS   Well;
　And well am like to do, for I perceive
73　Four feasts are toward.

POMPEY   Let me shake thy hand,
　I never hated thee: I have seen thee fight
　When I have envied thy behavior.

ENOBARBUS   Sir,
　I never loved you much; but I ha' praised ye
　When you have well deserved ten times as much
　As I have said you did.

POMPEY   Enjoy thy plainness,

73 *toward* coming up

It nothing ill becomes thee.   79
Aboard my galley I invite you all :
Will you lead, lords ?
ALL   Show's the way, sir.
POMPEY   Come.
Exeunt. Manent Enobarbus and Menas.
MENAS *[aside]* Thy father, Pompey, would ne'er have
    made this treaty. – You and I have known, sir.   83
ENOBARBUS At sea, I think.
MENAS We have, sir.
ENOBARBUS You have done well by water.
MENAS And you by land.
ENOBARBUS I will praise any man that will praise me;
    though it cannot be denied what I have done by land.
MENAS Nor what I have done by water.
ENOBARBUS Yes, something you can deny for your own
    safety : you have been a great thief by sea.
MENAS And you by land.
ENOBARBUS There I deny my land service. But give me
    your hand, Menas : if our eyes had authority, here they 95
    might take two thieves kissing.
MENAS All men's faces are true, whatsome'er their hands
    are.
ENOBARBUS But there is never a fair woman has a true 99
    face.
MENAS No slander, they steal hearts.
ENOBARBUS We came hither to fight with you.
MENAS For my part, I am sorry it is turned to a drinking.
    Pompey doth this day laugh away his fortune.
ENOBARBUS If he do, sure he cannot weep't back again.
MENAS Y' have said, sir. We looked not for Mark Antony 105
    here. Pray you, is he married to Cleopatra ?
ENOBARBUS Caesar's sister is called Octavia.
MENAS True, sir, she was the wife of Caius Marcellus.

79 *nothing* not at all   83 *known* met   95 *had* were in   99 *true* honest   105
Y' have said i.e. you are quite right

ENOBARBUS But she is now the wife of Marcus Antonius.

110 MENAS Pray ye, sir?

ENOBARBUS 'Tis true.

MENAS Then is Caesar and he for ever knit together.

ENOBARBUS If I were bound to divine of this unity, I would not prophesy so.

115 MENAS I think the policy of that purpose made more in the marriage than the love of the parties.

ENOBARBUS I think so too. But you shall find the band that seems to tie their friendship together will be the very strangler of their amity: Octavia is of a holy, cold,

120 and still conversation.

MENAS Who would not have his wife so?

ENOBARBUS Not he that himself is not so; which is Mark Antony. He will to his Egyptian dish again: then shall the sighs of Octavia blow the fire up in Caesar, and, as I said before, that which is the strength of their amity shall prove the immediate author of their variance. Antony

127 will use his affection where it is. He married but his

128 occasion here.

MENAS And thus it may be. Come, sir, will you aboard? I have a health for you.

ENOBARBUS I shall take it, sir: we have used our throats in Egypt.

MENAS Come, let's away.   *Exeunt.*

*

II, vii   *Music plays. Enter two or three Servants, with a banquet.*

1 1. SERVANT Here they'll be, man. Some o' their plants are ill-rooted already; the least wind i' th' world will blow them down.

---

110 *Pray ye* i.e. how's that again 115 *made more* played more part 120 *conversation* way of life 127 *where it is* i.e. in Egypt 128 *occasion* convenience
II, vii Aboard Pompey's galley in the port of Misenum 1 *plants* feet (with pun on the usual sense: cf. *ill-rooted*)

74

2. SERVANT Lepidus is high-colored.

1. SERVANT They have made him drink alms-drink. 5

2. SERVANT As they pinch one another by the disposition, he cries out 'No more,' reconciles them to his entreaty, and himself to th' drink. 7

1. SERVANT But it raises the greater war between him and his discretion.

2. SERVANT Why, this it is to have a name in great men's fellowship. I had as live have a reed that will do 12 me no service as a partisan I could not heave. 13

1. SERVANT To be called into a huge sphere and not to 14 be seen to move in't, are the holes where eyes should be, which pitifully disaster the cheeks. 16

A sennet sounded. Enter Caesar, Antony, Pompey, Lepidus, Agrippa, Maecenas, Enobarbus, Menas, with other Captains.

ANTONY
Thus do they, sir: they take the flow o' th' Nile
By certain scales i' th' pyramid. They know 18
By th' height, the lowness, or the mean, if dearth 19
Or foison follow. The higher Nilus swells,
The more it promises; as it ebbs, the seedsman
Upon the slime and ooze scatters his grain,
And shortly comes to harvest.

LEPIDUS Y' have strange serpents there.

ANTONY Ay, Lepidus.

LEPIDUS Your serpent of Egypt is bred now of your mud by the operation of your sun: so is your crocodile.

ANTONY They are so.

---

5 *alms-drink* drink drunk on behalf of one too far gone to continue his part in a round of toasts (Lepidus has been tricked into drinking more than the rest) **7** *No more* i.e. no more quarrelling **12** *live* lief **13** *partisan* spear **14–16** *To . . . cheeks* (Lepidus, a little man in a part too big for him, is compared first to a heavenly body that fails to perform its function in its *sphere*, and then to a face without eyes; *disaster*, carrying the image back on itself, likens the face without eyes to a heaven without stars) **16 s.d.** *sennet* distinctive set of trumpet notes announcing persons of importance **18** *scales* graduations **19–20** *dearth Or foison* famine or plenty

POMPEY Sit – and some wine ! A health to Lepidus !

30 LEPIDUS I am not so well as I should be, but I'll ne'er out.

31 ENOBARBUS Not till you have slept. I fear me you'll be in
till then.

33 LEPIDUS Nay, certainly, I have heard the Ptolemies' pyramises are very goodly things : without contradiction I
have heard that.

MENAS
Pompey, a word.

POMPEY   Say in mine ear. What is't ?

MENAS
Forsake thy seat, I do beseech thee, captain,
And hear me speak a word.

POMPEY   Forbear me till anon.
    [Menas] whispers in's ear.
This wine for Lepidus !

LEPIDUS What manner o' thing is your crocodile ?

ANTONY It is shaped, sir, like itself, and it is as broad as it
42   hath breadth ; it is just so high as it is, and moves with it
own organs. It lives by that which nourisheth it, and
44   the elements once out of it, it transmigrates.

LEPIDUS What color is it of ?

46 ANTONY Of it own color too.

LEPIDUS 'Tis a strange serpent.

48 ANTONY 'Tis so, and the tears of it are wet.

CAESAR Will this description satisfy him ?

ANTONY With the health that Pompey gives him ; else he
is a very epicure.
    [Menas whispers again.]
POMPEY
Go hang, sir, hang ! Tell me of that ? Away !
Do as I bid you. – Where's this cup I called for ?

30 *ne'er out* never give up   31 *in* drunk   33 *pyramises* (Lepidus's drunken
rendering of 'pyramides,' i.e. pyramids)   42–43, 46 *it own* its own   44
transmigrates i.e. its soul takes over the body of some other creature
(Antony is teasing the drunken Lepidus)   48 *tears* i.e. its 'crocodile tears'

MENAS
　If for the sake of merit thou wilt hear me,
　Rise from thy stool.
POMPEY　　　　　　I think th' art mad.
　　　[Rises and walks aside.]　　　　The matter?
MENAS
　I have ever held my cap off to thy fortunes.　　　56
POMPEY
　Thou hast served me with much faith. What's else to
　　say? –
　Be jolly, lords.
ANTONY　　　These quicksands, Lepidus,
　Keep off them, for you sink.
MENAS
　Wilt thou be lord of all the world?
POMPEY　　　　　　What say'st thou?
MENAS
　Wilt thou be lord of the whole world? That's twice.
POMPEY
　How should that be?
MENAS　　　　　But entertain it,　　　62
　And though thou think me poor, I am the man
　Will give thee all the world.
POMPEY　　　　　Hast thou drunk well?
MENAS
　No, Pompey, I have kept me from the cup.
　Thou art, if thou dar'st be, the earthly Jove:
　Whate'er the ocean pales, or sky inclips,　　　67
　Is thine, if thou wilt ha't.
POMPEY　　　　　Show me which way.
MENAS
　These three world-sharers, these competitors,　　　69
　Are in thy vessel. Let me cut the cable;
　And when we are put off, fall to their throats.
　All there is thine.

56 *held . . . off* i.e. been devoted　62 *But entertain it* only accept the idea
67 *pales* encloses　69 *competitors* partners

POMPEY   Ah, this thou shouldst have done,
    And not have spoke on't. In me 'tis villainy,
    In thee't had been good service. Thou must know,
    'Tis not my profit that does lead mine honor ;
76 Mine honor, it. Repent that e'er thy tongue
    Hath so betrayed thine act. Being done unknown,
    I should have found it afterwards well done,
    But must condemn it now. Desist, and drink.
MENAS [aside]
    For this,
81 I'll never follow thy palled fortunes more.
    Who seeks, and will not take when once 'tis offered,
    Shall never find it more.
POMPEY   This health to Lepidus !
ANTONY
84 Bear him ashore. I'll pledge it for him, Pompey.
ENOBARBUS
    Here's to thee, Menas.
MENAS   Enobarbus, welcome.
POMPEY Fill till the cup be hid.
ENOBARBUS There's a strong fellow, Menas.
        [Points to the Servant who carries off Lepidus.]
MENAS Why ?
ENOBARBUS 'A bears the third part of the world, man ;
    seest not ?
MENAS
    The third part then is drunk. Would it were all,
92 That it might go on wheels !
ENOBARBUS
93 Drink thou : increase the reels.
MENAS Come.
POMPEY
    This is not yet an Alexandrian feast.

---

76 *Mine honor, it* i.e. my honor comes before my profit   81 *palled* decayed
84 *I'll . . . him* (cf. l. 5: Antony is now taking an *alms-drink*)   92 *go on
wheels* whirl smoothly   93 *reels* whirls

ANTONY
   It ripens towards it. Strike the vessels, ho!   96
   Here's to Caesar!
CAESAR   I could well forbear't.   97
   It's monstrous labor when I wash my brain
   And it grows fouler.
ANTONY   Be a child o' th' time.   ← *seize the moment...*
CAESAR
   Possess it, I'll make answer;   *} you take time, don't*   100
   But I had rather fast from all four days   *let it take you*
   Than drink so much in one.
ENOBARBUS   Ha, my brave emperor!   *(as A.*
   Shall we dance now the Egyptian Bacchanals   *says above)*
   And celebrate our drink?
POMPEY   Let's ha't, good soldier.
ANTONY
   Come, let's all take hands
   Till that the conquering wine hath steeped our sense
   In soft and delicate Lethe.   107
ENOBARBUS   All take hands:
   Make battery to our ears with the loud music;
   The while I'll place you; then the boy shall sing.
   The holding every man shall bear as loud   110
   As his strong sides can volley.
      Music plays. Enobarbus places them hand in hand.

        The Song.

      Come, thou monarch of the vine,
      Plumpy Bacchus with pink eyne!   113
      In thy fats our cares be drowned,   114
      With thy grapes our hairs be crowned.
         Cup us till the world go round,
         Cup us till the world go round!

---

96 *Strike the vessels* broach the casks **97** *forbear't* i.e. pass up this toast
100 *Possess it* down it **107** *Lethe* (cf. II, i, 27n.) **110** *holding* refrain
113 *pink* half-closed **114** *fats* vats

CAESAR

What would you more ? Pompey, good night.
Good brother,
119   Let me request you off : our graver business
Frowns at this levity. Gentle lords, let's part ;
You see we have burned our cheeks. Strong Enobarb
Is weaker than the wine, and mine own tongue
123   Splits what it speaks : the wild disguise hath almost
124   Anticked us all. What needs more words ? Good night.
Good Antony, your hand.
125 POMPEY   I'll try you on the shore.

ANTONY

And shall, sir. – Give's your hand.

POMPEY   O Antony,
You have my father's house. But what, we are friends !
Come down into the boat.

ENOBARBUS   Take heed you fall not.
                    [Exeunt all but Enobarbus and Menas.]
Menas, I'll not on shore.

MENAS   No, to my cabin.
These drums ! these trumpets, flutes ! what !
Let Neptune hear we bid a loud farewell
To these great fellows. Sound and be hanged, sound
    out !
        Sound a flourish, with drums.

ENOBARBUS

Hoo ! says 'a. There's my cap.

MENAS

Hoo ! Noble captain, come.   *Exeunt.*

*

119 *off* to come away   123 *disguise* dancing and drinking   124 *Anticked*
made fools of   125 *try you* take you on in a drinking bout

ANTONY AND CLEOPATRA

Enter Ventidius as it were in triumph, the dead body   III, i
of Pacorus borne before him [by Romans].

VENTIDIUS

Now, darting Parthia, art thou struck, and now   1
Pleased fortune does of Marcus Crassus' death
Make me revenger. Bear the King's son's body
Before our army. Thy Pacorus, Orodes,
Pays this for Marcus Crassus.   5

ROMAN [SILIUS]   Noble Ventidius,
Whilst yet with Parthian blood thy sword is warm,
The fugitive Parthians follow. Spur through Media,
Mesopotamia, and the shelters whither
The routed fly: so thy grand captain, Antony,
Shall set thee on triumphant chariots and
Put garlands on thy head.

VENTIDIUS   O Silius, Silius,
I have done enough. A lower place, note well,   12
May make too great an act. For learn this, Silius,
Better to leave undone, than by our deed
Acquire too high a fame when him we serve's away.
Caesar and Antony have ever won
More in their officer than person. Sossius,
One of my place in Syria, his lieutenant,
For quick accumulation of renown,
Which he achieved by th' minute, lost his favor.
Who does i' th' wars more than his captain can
Becomes his captain's captain; and ambition
(The soldier's virtue) rather makes choice of loss
Than gain which darkens him.
I could do more to do Antonius good,
But 'twould offend him. And in his offense   26
Should my performance perish.

III, i A field in Syria   1 *darting* i.e. famous for its bowmen   5 *Marcus Crassus* (member of the first triumvirate with Pompey the Great and Julius Caesar, who was killed by the Parthians and who is now avenged by the death of Pacorus, son to Orodes the Parthian king)   12 *A lower place* an underling   26 *in his offense* in offending him

81

27 ROMAN [SILIUS]   Thou hast, Ventidius, that
Without the which a soldier and his sword
Grants scarce distinction. Thou wilt write to Antony?

VENTIDIUS
I'll humbly signify what in his name,
That magical word of war, we have effected;
How with his banners and his well-paid ranks
The ne'er-yet-beaten horse of Parthia
34 We have jaded out o' th' field.

ROMAN [SILIUS]   Where is he now?

VENTIDIUS
He purposeth to Athens; whither, with what haste
The weight we must convey with's will permit,
We shall appear before him. – On, there, pass along.
                                                                Exeunt

                              *

III, ii   *Enter Agrippa at one door, Enobarbus at another.*

AGRIPPA
1   What, are the brothers parted?

ENOBARBUS
They have dispatched with Pompey; he is gone;
3   The other three are sealing. Octavia weeps
To part from Rome; Caesar is sad, and Lepidus
Since Pompey's feast, as Menas says, is troubled
6   With the green-sickness.

AGRIPPA   'Tis a noble Lepidus.

ENOBARBUS
A very fine one. O, how he loves Caesar!

AGRIPPA
Nay, but how dearly he adores Mark Antony!

---

27 *that* i.e. discretion   34 *jaded* driven weary
III, ii The house of Octavius Caesar in Rome   1 *parted* departed   3
sealing concluding agreements   6 *green-sickness* (traditionally the disease
of lovesick girls: Lepidus is likened to one in his relations to Caesar and
Antony)

ENOBARBUS
Caesar? Why, he's the Jupiter of men.
AGRIPPA
What's Antony? The god of Jupiter.
ENOBARBUS
Spake you of Caesar? How! the nonpareil!
AGRIPPA
O Antony! O thou Arabian bird! 12
ENOBARBUS
Would you praise Caesar, say 'Caesar': go no further.
AGRIPPA
Indeed he plied them both with excellent praises.
ENOBARBUS
But he loves Caesar best, yet he loves Antony:
Hoo! hearts, tongues, figures, scribes, bards, poets,
cannot
Think, speak, cast, write, sing, number – hoo! –
His love to Antony. But as for Caesar,
Kneel down, kneel down, and wonder.
AGRIPPA   Both he loves.
ENOBARBUS
They are his shards, and he their beetle. 20
    [Trumpet within.]   So –
This is to horse. Adieu, noble Agrippa.
AGRIPPA
Good fortune, worthy soldier, and farewell!
    Enter Caesar, Antony, Lepidus, and Octavia.
ANTONY
No further, sir.
CAESAR
You take from me a great part of myself;
Use me well in't. Sister, prove such a wife
As my thoughts make thee, and as my farthest band 26

12 *Arabian bird* i.e. unique (like the mythical phoenix, of which only one
was supposed to exist at a time) 20 *shards* wings 26–27 *as my farthest ...
approof* such as I will give my uttermost bond that you will prove to be

Shall pass on thy approof. Most noble Antony,
28   Let not the piece of virtue which is set
Betwixt us as the cement of our love
To keep it builded, be the ram to batter
The fortress of it : for better might we
32   Have loved without this mean, if on both parts
This be not cherished.

ANTONY   Make me not offended
In your distrust.

CAESAR   I have said.

ANTONY   You shall not find,
35   Though you be therein curious, the least cause
For what you seem to fear. So the gods keep you
And make the hearts of Romans serve your ends !
We will here part.

CAESAR

Farewell, my dearest sister, fare thee well.
The elements be kind to thee, and make
Thy spirits all of comfort : fare thee well.

OCTAVIA

My noble brother !

ANTONY   ✳ ♥

The April 's in her eyes : it is love's spring,
And these the showers to bring it on. Be cheerful.

OCTAVIA

Sir, look well to my husband's house ; and –

CAESAR   What,
Octavia ?

OCTAVIA   I'll tell you in your ear.

ANTONY

Her tongue will not obey her heart, nor can
48   Her heart inform her tongue – the swan's down-feather
That stands upon the swell at full of tide,
And neither way inclines.

---

28 *piece* paragon   **32** *mean* intermediary   **35** *curious* punctiliously exacting
48–50 *the swan's . . . inclines* i.e. her feelings for husband and brother are
evenly balanced

ENOBARBUS
    Will Caesar weep?   51

AGRIPPA   He has a cloud in's face.

ENOBARBUS
    He were the worse for that, were he a horse;   52
    So is he, being a man.

AGRIPPA   Why, Enobarbus,
    When Antony found Julius Caesar dead,
    He cried almost to roaring; and he wept
    When at Philippi he found Brutus slain.

ENOBARBUS
    That year indeed he was troubled with a rheum.   57
    What willingly he did confound he wailed,   58
    Believe't, till I wept too.

CAESAR   No, sweet Octavia,
    You shall hear from me still: the time shall not   60
    Outgo my thinking on you.

ANTONY   Come, sir, come,
    I'll wrestle with you in my strength of love:
    Look, here I have you; thus I let you go,
    And give you to the gods.

CAESAR   Adieu, be happy!

LEPIDUS
    Let all the number of the stars give light
    To thy fair way!

CAESAR   Farewell, farewell!
      Kisses Octavia.

ANTONY   Farewell!
                 Trumpets sound. Exeunt.

*

51–59 (Enobarbus and Agrippa talk aside)   52 *horse* (horses without white markings on the face were thought to be ill-tempered)   57 *rheum* running at the eyes   58 *confound* destroy   60–61 *the time . . . you* i.e. my thoughts of you will not be left behind (as in a race) by time

III, iii   *Enter Cleopatra, Charmian, Iras, and Alexas.*

CLEOPATRA
Where is the fellow?

ALEXAS   Half afeard to come.

CLEOPATRA
Go to, go to.
                Enter the Messenger as before.
                          Come hither, sir.

ALEXAS   Good Majesty,
3   Herod of Jewry dare not look upon you
But when you are well pleased.

CLEOPATRA   That Herod's head
I'll have: but how, when Antony is gone
Through whom I might command it? Come thou near.

MESSENGER
Most gracious Majesty!

CLEOPATRA
Didst thou behold Octavia?

MESSENGER Ay, dread Queen.

CLEOPATRA Where.

MESSENGER
Madam, in Rome.
I looked her in the face, and saw her led
Between her brother and Mark Antony.

CLEOPATRA
Is she as tall as me?

MESSENGER   She is not, madam.

CLEOPATRA
Didst hear her speak? Is she shrill-tongued or low?

MESSENGER
Madam, I heard her speak; she is low-voiced.

CLEOPATRA
17   That's not so good. He cannot like her long.

CHARMIAN
Like her? O Isis! 'tis impossible.

III, iii The chambers of Cleopatra in her palace at Alexandria   3 *Herod* i.e.
even Herod (traditionally represented as a tyrant)   17 *good* i.e. as I am

CLEOPATRA
    I think so, Charmian. Dull of tongue, and dwarfish.
    What majesty is in her gait? Remember,
    If e'er thou lookedst on majesty.
MESSENGER   She creeps:
    Her motion and her station are as one.   22
    She shows a body rather than a life,
    A statue than a breather.
CLEOPATRA   Is this certain?
MESSENGER
    Or I have no observance.
CHARMIAN   Three in Egypt
    Cannot make better note.
CLEOPATRA   He's very knowing,
    I do perceive't. There's nothing in her yet.
    The fellow has good judgment.
CHARMIAN   Excellent.
CLEOPATRA
    Guess at her years, I prithee.
MESSENGER   Madam,
    She was a widow –
CLEOPATRA   Widow? Charmian, hark.
MESSENGER
    And I do think she's thirty.
CLEOPATRA
    Bear'st thou her face in mind? is't long or round?   32
MESSENGER
    Round even to faultiness.
CLEOPATRA
    For the most part, too, they are foolish that are so.
    Her hair, what color?
MESSENGER
    Brown, madam; and her forehead
    As low as she would wish it.
CLEOPATRA   There's gold for thee.

22 *Her . . . one* even in motion she is still   32 *long or round* (thought to be
signs, respectively, of prudence and folly)

Thou must not take my former sharpness ill;
I will employ thee back again : I find thee
Most fit for business. Go, make thee ready;
Our letters are prepared.   *[Exit Messenger.]*

41 CHARMIAN   A proper man.

CLEOPATRA

Indeed he is so : I repent me much
43 That so I harried him. Why, methinks, by him,
44 This creature 's no such thing.

CHARMIAN   Nothing, madam.

CLEOPATRA

The man hath seen some majesty, and should know.

CHARMIAN

Hath he seen majesty ? Isis else defend,
And serving you so long !

CLEOPATRA

I have one thing more to ask him yet, good Charmian ;
But 'tis no matter, thou shalt bring him to me
Where I will write. All may be well enough.

CHARMIAN

I warrant you, madam.   *Exeunt.*

*

III, iv   *Enter Antony and Octavia.*

ANTONY

Nay, nay, Octavia, not only that,
That were excusable, that and thousands more
3 Of semblable import – but he hath waged
4 New wars 'gainst Pompey ; made his will, and read it
To public ear ;
Spoke scantly of me : when perforce he could not
But pay me terms of honor, cold and sickly
8 He vented them, most narrow measure lent me ;

41 *proper* attractive   43 *harried* mistreated   44 *no such thing* nothing much
III, iv The house of Antony in Athens   3 *semblable* like   4 *read it* (to
show the public what benefactions they might expect from him)   8
narrow measure little credit

When the best hint was given him, he not took't,
Or did it from his teeth.   10

OCTAVIA   O, my good lord,
Believe not all, or if you must believe,
Stomach not all. A more unhappy lady,   12
If this division chance, ne'er stood between,
Praying for both parts.
The good gods will mock me presently   15
When I shall pray 'O, bless my lord and husband!'
Undo that prayer by crying out as loud
'O, bless my brother!' Husband win, win brother,
Prays, and destroys the prayer; no midway
'Twixt these extremes at all.

ANTONY   Gentle Octavia,
Let your best love draw to that point which seeks
Best to preserve it. If I lose mine honor,
I lose myself: better I were not yours
Than yours so branchless. But as you requested,   24
Yourself shall go between's: the mean time, lady,
I'll raise the preparation of a war
Shall stain your brother. Make your soonest haste;   27
So your desires are yours.

OCTAVIA   Thanks to my lord.
The Jove of power make me most weak, most weak,
Your reconciler! Wars 'twixt you twain would be
As if the world should cleave, and that slain men
Should solder up the rift.

ANTONY
When it appears to you where this begins,
Turn your displeasure that way, for our faults
Can never be so equal that your love
Can equally move with them. Provide your going;
Choose your own company, and command what cost
Your heart has mind to.   *Exeunt.*

10 *from his teeth* grudgingly   12 *Stomach* resent   15 *presently* at once
24 *branchless* pruned (of my honors)   27 *stain* eclipse

III, v   *Enter Enobarbus and Eros.*

ENOBARBUS How now, friend Eros?

EROS There's strange news come, sir.

ENOBARBUS What, man?

EROS Caesar and Lepidus have made wars upon Pompey.

5 ENOBARBUS This is old. What is the success?

6 EROS Caesar, having made use of him in the wars 'gainst
7   Pompey, presently denied him rivality, would not let
     him partake in the glory of the action; and not resting
     here, accuses him of letters he had formerly wrote to
10   Pompey; upon his own appeal, seizes him; so the poor
11   third is up till death enlarge his confine.

ENOBARBUS
12   Then, world, thou hast a pair of chaps, no more;
     And throw between them all the food thou hast,
     They'll grind the one the other. Where's Antony?

EROS
     He's walking in the garden – thus, and spurns
     The rush that lies before him; cries 'Fool Lepidus!'
17   And threats the throat of that his officer
     That murd'red Pompey.

ENOBARBUS   Our great navy 's rigged.

EROS
     For Italy and Caesar. More, Domitius:
     My lord desires you presently. My news
     I might have told hereafter.

ENOBARBUS   'Twill be naught;
     But let it be. Bring me to Antony.

EROS Come, sir.   *Exeunt.*

*

III, v **5** *success* sequel **6** *wars* (a new outbreak, in which Pompey was
defeated) **7** *rivality* partnership **10** *appeal* accusation **11** *up* jailed
12 *chaps* jaws **17** *that his officer* that officer of his

Enter Agrippa, Maecenas, and Caesar. III, vi

CAESAR

Contemning Rome, he has done all this and more 1
In Alexandria. Here's the manner of't :
I' th' market place on a tribunal silvered,
Cleopatra and himself in chairs of gold
Were publicly enthroned ; at the feet sat
Caesarion, whom they call my father's son, 6
And all the unlawful issue that their lust
Since then hath made between them. Unto her
He gave the stablishment of Egypt ; made her 9
Of lower Syria, Cyprus, Lydia,
Absolute queen.

MAECENAS   This in the public eye ?

CAESAR

I' th' common show-place, where they exercise.
His sons he there proclaimed the kings of kings :
Great Media, Parthia, and Armenia
He gave to Alexander ; to Ptolemy he assigned
Syria, Cilicia, and Phoenicia. She
In th' habiliments of the goddess Isis 17
That day appeared, and oft before gave audience,
As 'tis reported, so.

MAECENAS   Let Rome be thus
Informed.

AGRIPPA   Who, queasy with his insolence 20
Already, will their good thoughts call from him.

CAESAR

The people know it, and have now received
His accusations.

AGRIPPA   Who does he accuse ?

CAESAR

Caesar, and that, having in Sicily

III, vi The house of Octavius Caesar in Rome   1 *Contemning* scorning
6 *my father's* (Octavius, though actually a nephew, had been adopted by
Julius Caesar)   9 *stablishment* rule   17 *Isis* (cf. I, ii, 60n.)   20 *queasy*
nauseated

25   Sextus Pompeius spoiled, we had not rated him
26   His part o' th' isle. Then does he say he lent me
     Some shipping unrestored. Lastly, he frets
     That Lepidus of the triumvirate
     Should be deposed; and, being, that we detain
     All his revenue.

AGRIPPA   Sir, this should be answered.

CAESAR
     'Tis done already, and the messenger gone.
     I have told him Lepidus was grown too cruel,
     That he his high authority abused
     And did deserve his change. For what I have conquered,
     I grant him part; but then in his Armenia,
     And other of his conquered kingdoms, I
     Demand the like.

MAECENAS   He'll never yield to that.

CAESAR
     Nor must not then be yielded to in this.
         Enter Octavia with her Train.

OCTAVIA
     Hail, Caesar, and my lord, hail, most dear Caesar!

CAESAR
40   That ever I should call thee castaway!

OCTAVIA
     You have not called me so, nor have you cause.

CAESAR
     Why have you stol'n upon us thus? You come not
     Like Caesar's sister. The wife of Antony
     Should have an army for an usher, and
     The neighs of horse to tell of her approach
     Long ere she did appear. The trees by th' way
     Should have borne men, and expectation fainted,
     Longing for what it had not. Nay, the dust
     Should have ascended to the roof of heaven,

25 *spoiled* despoiled; *rated* allotted   **26** *isle* i.e. Sicily

Raised by your populous troops. But you are come
A market-maid to Rome, and have prevented
The ostentation of our love; which, left unshown,
Is often left unloved. We should have met you   53
By sea and land, supplying every stage
With an augmented greeting.

OCTAVIA   Good my lord,
To come thus was I not constrained, but did it
On my free will. My lord, Mark Antony,
Hearing that you prepared for war, acquainted
My grievèd ear withal; whereon I begged
His pardon for return.

CAESAR   Which soon he granted,
Being an abstract 'tween his lust and him.   61

OCTAVIA
Do not say so, my lord.

CAESAR   I have eyes upon him,
And his affairs come to me on the wind.
Where is he now?

OCTAVIA   My lord, in Athens.

CAESAR
No, my most wrongèd sister, Cleopatra
Hath nodded him to her. He hath given his empire
Up to a whore, who now are levying
The kings o' th' earth for war. He hath assembled
Bocchus, the king of Libya; Archelaus,
Of Cappadocia; Philadelphos, king
Of Paphlagonia; the Thracian king, Adallas;
King Mauchus of Arabia; King of Pont;   72
Herod of Jewry; Mithridates, king
Of Comagene; Polemon and Amyntas,
The kings of Mede and Lycaonia; with a
More larger list of sceptres.

53 *left unloved* thought to be unfelt   61 *abstract* short-cut   72 *Mauchus*
(so spelled in folio; Plutarch reads 'Malchus,' and North's translation
'Manchus')

OCTAVIA   Ay me most wretched,
That have my heart parted betwixt two friends
That do afflict each other!
CAESAR   Welcome hither.
Your letters did withhold our breaking forth,
Till we perceived both how you were wrong led
81   And we in negligent danger. Cheer your heart:
Be you not troubled with the time, which drives
O'er your content these strong necessities;
But let determined things to destiny
Hold unbewailed their way. Welcome to Rome,
86   Nothing more dear to me. You are abused
87   Beyond the mark of thought: and the high gods,
88   To do you justice, makes his ministers
Of us and those that love you. Best of comfort,
And ever welcome to us.
AGRIPPA   Welcome, lady.
MAECENAS
Welcome, dear madam.
Each heart in Rome does love and pity you.
93   Only th' adulterous Antony, most large
In his abominations, turns you off
95   And gives his potent regiment to a trull
96   That noises it against us.
OCTAVIA   Is it so, sir?
CAESAR
Most certain. Sister, welcome. Pray you
98   Be ever known to patience. My dear'st sister!   *Exeunt.*

*

81 *negligent danger* danger through negligence   86 *abused* betrayed (by
Antony)   87 *mark* reach   88 *makes his* make their   93 *large* uninhibited
95 *regiment* rule; *trull* harlot   96 *noises it* clamors   98 *Be . . . patience* be
always calm

94

Enter Cleopatra and Enobarbus.   III, vii

CLEOPATRA
I will be even with thee, doubt it not.

ENOBARBUS
But why, why, why?

CLEOPATRA
Thou hast forspoke my being in these wars,   3
And say'st it is not fit.

ENOBARBUS   Well, is it, is it?

CLEOPATRA
Is't not denounced against us? Why should not we   5
Be there in person?

ENOBARBUS *[aside]* Well, I could reply:
If we should serve with horse and mares together,
The horse were merely lost; the mares would bear   8
A soldier and his horse.

CLEOPATRA   What is't you say?

ENOBARBUS
Your presence needs must puzzle Antony;   10
Take from his heart, take from his brain, from's time,
What should not then be spared. He is already
Traduced for levity; and 'tis said in Rome
That Photinus an eunuch and your maids
Manage this war.

CLEOPATRA   Sink Rome, and their tongues rot
That speak against us! A charge we bear i' th' war, 16
And as the president of my kingdom will
Appear there for a man. Speak not against it,
I will not stay behind.

      Enter Antony and Canidius.

ENOBARBUS   Nay, I have done.
Here comes the Emperor.

ANTONY   Is it not strange, Canidius,
That from Tarentum and Brundusium

III, vii Antony's camp near Actium   3 *forspoke* opposed   5 *denounced*
declared 8 *merely* entirely 10 *puzzle* paralyze 16 *charge* responsibility

He could so quickly cut the Ionian sea
23   And take in Toryne? – You have heard on't, sweet?

CLEOPATRA
Celerity is never more admired
Than by the negligent.

ANTONY   A good rebuke,
Which might have well becomed the best of men
To taunt at slackness. Canidius, we
Will fight with him by sea.

CLEOPATRA   By sea; what else?

CANIDIUS
Why will my lord do so?

29 ANTONY   For that he dares us to't.

ENOBARBUS
So hath my lord dared him to single fight.

CANIDIUS
Ay, and to wage this battle at Pharsalia,
Where Caesar fought with Pompey. But these offers,
Which serve not for his vantage, he shakes off;
And so should you.

ENOBARBUS   Your ships are not well manned;
35   Your mariners are muleters, reapers, people
36   Ingrossed by swift impress. In Caesar's fleet
Are those that often have 'gainst Pompey fought;
38   Their ships are yare; yours, heavy: no disgrace
39   Shall fall you for refusing him at sea,
Being prepared for land.

ANTONY   By sea, by sea.

ENOBARBUS
Most worthy sir, you therein throw away
The absolute soldiership you have by land,
43   Distract your army, which doth most consist
Of war-marked footmen, leave unexecuted
Your own renownèd knowledge, quite forgo

---

23 *take in* seize   29 *For that* because   35 *muleters* mule-drivers, i.e.
peasants   36 *Ingrossed* collected wholesale; *impress* draft   38 *yare* nimble
39 *you* to you   43 *Distract* divide

The way which promises assurance, and
Give up yourself merely to chance and hazard
From firm security.
ANTONY   I'll fight at sea.
CLEOPATRA
I have sixty sails, Caesar none better.
ANTONY
Our overplus of shipping will we burn,
And with the rest full-manned, from th' head of Actium
Beat th' approaching Caesar. But if we fail,
We then can do't at land.
          Enter a Messenger. Thy business?
MESSENGER
The news is true, my lord, he is descried;
Caesar has taken Toryne.
ANTONY
Can he be there in person? 'Tis impossible;
Strange that his power should be. Canidius,   57
Our nineteen legions thou shalt hold by land
And our twelve thousand horse. We'll to our ship.
Away, my Thetis!   60
          Enter a Soldier. How now, worthy soldier?
SOLDIER
O noble Emperor, do not fight by sea,
Trust not to rotten planks. Do you misdoubt
This sword and these my wounds? Let th' Egyptians
And the Phoenicians go a-ducking: we
Have used to conquer standing on the earth
And fighting foot to foot.
ANTONY   Well, well, away!
          Exit Antony [with] Cleopatra and Enobarbus.
SOLDIER
By Hercules, I think I am i' th' right.
CANIDIUS
Soldier, thou art; but his whole action grows   68

57 *power* army   60 *Thetis* name of a sea goddess   68–69 *his . . . on't* his plan
of action does not spring from a right estimate of the nature of his strength

97

Not in the power on't: so our leader's led,
And we are women's men.

SOLDIER   You keep by land
The legions and the horse whole, do you not?

CANIDIUS
Marcus Octavius, Marcus Justeius,
Publicola, and Caelius are for sea;
But we keep whole by land. This speed of Caesar's
75 Carries beyond belief.

SOLDIER   While he was yet in Rome,
76 His power went out in such distractions as
77 Beguiled all spies.

CANIDIUS   Who's his lieutenant, hear you?

SOLDIER
They say, one Taurus.

CANIDIUS   Well I know the man.
Enter a Messenger.

MESSENGER
The Emperor calls Canidius.

CANIDIUS
80 With news the time's with labor and throws forth
Each minute some.   *Exeunt.*

*

III, viii   *Enter Caesar, with his Army, marching.*

CAESAR Taurus!
TAURUS My lord?
CAESAR
Strike not by land; keep whole, provoke not battle
Till we have done at sea. Do not exceed
The prescript of this scroll. Our fortune lies
6 Upon this jump.   *Exit [with Taurus and the Army].*

75 *Carries* i.e. like an arrow 76 *distractions* detachments 77 *Beguiled* deceived 80 *throws* i.e. as an animal 'throws,' gives birth to, its young III, viii A field near Actium 6 *jump* chance

Enter Antony and Enobarbus.   III, ix

ANTONY

Set we our squadrons on yond side o' th' hill
In eye of Caesar's battle; from which place   2
We may the number of the ships behold,
And so proceed accordingly.   *Exit [with Enobarbus].*

Canidius marcheth with his land army one way over   III, x
the stage, and Taurus, the lieutenant of Caesar, the
other way. After their going in is heard the noise of a
sea-fight. Alarum. Enter Enobarbus.

ENOBARBUS

Naught, naught, all naught! I can behold no longer.   1
Th' Antoniad, the Egyptian admiral,   2
With all their sixty, fly and turn the rudder:
To see't mine eyes are blasted.
                    Enter Scarus.

SCARUS   Gods and goddesses,
All the whole synod of them!   5

ENOBARBUS   What's thy passion?

SCARUS

The greater cantle of the world is lost   6
With very ignorance; we have kissed away
Kingdoms and provinces.

ENOBARBUS   How appears the fight?

SCARUS

On our side like the tokened pestilence   9
Where death is sure. Yon ribaudred nag of Egypt –   10
Whom leprosy o'ertake! – i' th' midst o' th' fight,
When vantage like a pair of twins appeared,
Both as the same, or rather ours the elder,   13
The breese upon her, like a cow in June,   14
Hoists sails, and flies.

III, ix 2 *battle* battle-line
III, x 1 *Naught* i.e. all's come to naught 2 *admiral* flagship 5 *synod*
assembly 6 *cantle* piece 9 *like . . . pestilence* like the plague when its
certain symptoms have been seen 10 *ribaudred* foul, obscene (many
editors read 'ribald-rid,' but the meaning is the same) 13 *elder* i.e.
superior 14 *breese* stinging fly (with pun on 'breeze')

ENOBARBUS
    That I beheld :
    Mine eyes did sicken at the sight, and could not
    Endure a further view.
18 SCARUS   She once being loofed,
    The noble ruin of her magic, Antony,
20   Claps on his sea-wing, and (like a doting mallard)
    Leaving the fight in heighth, flies after her.
    I never saw an action of such shame;
    Experience, manhood, honor, ne'er before
    Did violate so itself.
ENOBARBUS   Alack, alack!
    Enter Canidius.
CANIDIUS
    Our fortune on the sea is out of breath,
    And sinks most lamentably. Had our general
27   Been what he knew himself, it had gone well.
    O, he has given example for our flight
    Most grossly by his own.
29 ENOBARBUS   Ay, are you thereabouts?
    Why then, good night indeed.
CANIDIUS
    Toward Peloponnesus are they fled.
SCARUS
    'Tis easy to't; and there I will attend
    What further comes.
CANIDIUS   To Caesar will I render
    My legions and my horse; six kings already
    Show me the way of yielding.
ENOBARBUS   I'll yet follow
36   The wounded chance of Antony, though my reason
37   Sits in the wind against me.   *[Exeunt.]*

*

18 *loofed* luffed, turned to the wind to fly (?), disengaged (?)   20 *doting mallard* lovesick wild duck   27 *what . . . himself* his true self (as a great soldier)   29 *are you thereabouts* i.e. is that where your thoughts are   36 *chance* fortunes   37 *Sits . . . me* dissuades me

Enter Antony with Attendants.　　　　　　　　III, xi

ANTONY

Hark! the land bids me tread no more upon't,
It is ashamed to bear me. Friends, come hither.
I am so lated in the world that I　　　　　　　　3
Have lost my way for ever. I have a ship
Laden with gold: take that, divide it. Fly,
And make your peace with Caesar.

OMNES　　　　　　　　　　　　　　Fly? Not we.

ANTONY

I have fled myself, and have instructed cowards
To run and show their shoulders. Friends, be gone.
I have myself resolved upon a course
Which has no need of you. Be gone.
My treasure's in the harbor. Take it! O,
I followed that I blush to look upon.　　　　　　12
My very hairs do mutiny: for the white
Reprove the brown for rashness, and they them
For fear and doting. Friends, be gone, you shall
Have letters from me to some friends that will
Sweep your way for you. Pray you look not sad　17
Nor make replies of loathness; take the hint
Which my despair proclaims. Let that be left　　19
Which leaves itself. To the seaside straightway!
I will possess you of that ship and treasure.
Leave me, I pray, a little: pray you now,
Nay, do so; for indeed I have lost command,　　23
Therefore I pray you. I'll see you by and by.

　　　Sits down.
　　　Enter Cleopatra led by Charmian, [Iras,] and Eros.

EROS Nay, gentle madam, to him, comfort him.

IRAS Do, most dear Queen.

CHARMIAN Do? Why, what else?

III, xi The palace of Cleopatra in Alexandria　**3** *so . . . world* i.e. like a traveller after nightfall　**12** *that* what　**17** *Sweep* i.e. with Caesar　**19** *that* i.e. himself　**23–24** *I . . . pray you* i.e. I have lost the right to order you, so I entreat you

CLEOPATRA Let me sit down. O Juno!

ANTONY No, no, no, no, no.

EROS See you here, sir?

ANTONY O fie, fie, fie!

CHARMIAN Madam!

IRAS Madam, O good Empress!

EROS Sir, sir!

ANTONY

35   Yes, my lord, yes. He at Philippi kept
        His sword e'en like a dancer, while I struck
        The lean and wrinkled Cassius; and 'twas I
        That the mad Brutus ended: he alone
39   Dealt on lieutenantry, and no practice had
40   In the brave squares of war: yet now – No matter.

CLEOPATRA Ah, stand by.

EROS The Queen, my lord, the Queen.

IRAS

        Go to him, madam, speak to him;
44   He is unqualitied with very shame.

CLEOPATRA

        Well then, sustain me. O!

EROS

        Most noble sir, arise. The Queen approaches.
47   Her head's declined, and death will seize her, but
        Your comfort makes the rescue.

ANTONY

        I have offended reputation,
        A most unnoble swerving.

EROS   Sir, the Queen.

ANTONY

        O, whither hast thou led me, Egypt? See
        How I convey my shame out of thine eyes

35–36 *kept . . . dancer* i.e. never drew his sword 39 *Dealt on lieutenantry*
relied on subordinates 40 *squares* squadrons 44 *unqualitied* unmanned
47 *but* unless

By looking back what I have left behind   53
'Stroyed in dishonor.

CLEOPATRA   O my lord, my lord,
Forgive my fearful sails: I little thought
You would have followed.

ANTONY   Egypt, thou knew'st too well
My heart was to thy rudder tied by th' strings,
And thou shouldst tow me after. O'er my spirit
Thy full supremacy thou knew'st, and that
Thy beck might from the bidding of the gods   60
Command me.

CLEOPATRA   O, my pardon!

ANTONY   Now I must
To the young man send humble treaties, dodge   62
And palter in the shifts of lowness, who   63
With half the bulk o' th' world played as I pleased,
Making and marring fortunes. You did know
How much you were my conqueror, and that
My sword, made weak by my affection, would
Obey it on all cause.

CLEOPATRA   Pardon, pardon!

ANTONY
Fall not a tear, I say: one of them rates   69
All that is won and lost. Give me a kiss;
Even this repays me. We sent our schoolmaster.   71
Is 'a come back? Love, I am full of lead.   72
Some wine, within there, and our viands! Fortune
    knows
We scorn her most when most she offers blows. *Exeunt.*

*

53 *By looking back* i.e. by averting my eyes from yours and looking back at
60 *beck* beckoning   62 *treaties* proposals   63 *palter . . . lowness* i.e. use
the tricks to which a man brought low is reduced   69 *Fall* let fall; *rates*
equals   71 *schoolmaster* i.e. his children's tutor   72 *lead* i.e. grief

III, xii   *Enter Caesar, Agrippa, Dolabella, [Thidias,]*
      with others.

CAESAR
  Let him appear that's come from Antony.
  Know you him?

DOLABELLA   Caesar, 'tis his schoolmaster:
  An argument that he is plucked, when hither
  He sends so poor a pinion of his wing,
  Which had superfluous kings for messengers
  Not many moons gone by.
     Enter Ambassador from Antony.

CAESAR   Approach and speak.

AMBASSADOR
  Such as I am, I come from Antony.
  I was of late as petty to his ends
  As is the morn-dew on the myrtle leaf
10   To his grand sea.

CAESAR   Be't so. Declare thine office.

AMBASSADOR
  Lord of his fortunes he salutes thee, and
12   Requires to live in Egypt; which not granted,
13   He lessons his requests, and to thee sues
14   To let him breathe between the heavens and earth,
  A private man in Athens: this for him.
  Next, Cleopatra does confess thy greatness,
  Submits her to thy might, and of thee craves
18   The circle of the Ptolemies for her heirs,
19   Now hazarded to thy grace.

CAESAR   For Antony,
  I have no ears to his request. The Queen
21   Of audience nor desire shall fail, so she
  From Egypt drive her all-disgracèd friend
  Or take his life there. This if she perform,

III, xii The camp of Octavius Caesar in Egypt   10 *sea* i.e. the ultimate
source of dew   12 *Requires* requests   13 *lessons* disciplines   14 *breathe*
i.e. go on living   18 *circle* crown   19 *hazarded . . . grace* dependent on
your mercy   21 *audience* a hearing; *so* provided

She shall not sue unheard. So to them both.
AMBASSADOR
Fortune pursue thee!
CAESAR   Bring him through the bands.   25
                              [Exit Ambassador.]
    [To Thidias]
To try thy eloquence now 'tis time. Dispatch.
From Antony win Cleopatra: promise,
And in our name, what she requires; add more,
From thine invention, offers. Women are not
In their best fortunes strong, but want will perjure
The ne'er-touched Vestal. Try thy cunning, Thidias;
Make thine own edict for thy pains, which we   32
Will answer as a law.
THIDIAS   Caesar, I go.
CAESAR
Observe how Antony becomes his flaw,   34
And what thou think'st his very action speaks   35
In every power that moves.
THIDIAS   Caesar, I shall.   *Exeunt.*

*

    Enter Cleopatra, Enobarbus, Charmian, and Iras. III, xiii
CLEOPATRA
What shall we do, Enobarbus?
ENOBARBUS   Think, and die.
CLEOPATRA
Is Antony or we in fault for this?
ENOBARBUS
Antony only, that would make his will   3
Lord of his reason. What though you fled
From that great face of war, whose several ranges   5

25 *bands* troops   32 *Make . . . edict* name your own price (as reward)
34 *becomes his flaw* takes his fall   35-36 *And . . . moves* and what you think
his every move reveals
III, xiii The palace of Cleopatra   3 *will* desire   5 *ranges* battle-lines

Frighted each other? Why should he follow?
The itch of his affection should not then
8 Have nicked his captainship, at such a point,
When half to half the world opposed, he being
10 The merèd question. 'Twas a shame no less
11 Than was his loss, to course your flying flags
And leave his navy gazing.

CLEOPATRA   Prithee peace.

Enter the Ambassador, with Antony.

ANTONY
Is that his answer?

AMBASSADOR
Ay, my lord.

ANTONY
The Queen shall then have courtesy, so she
Will yield us up.

AMBASSADOR   He says so.

ANTONY   Let her know't.
To the boy Caesar send this grizzled head,
And he will fill thy wishes to the brim
With principalities.

CLEOPATRA   That head, my lord?

ANTONY
To him again! Tell him he wears the rose
Of youth upon him; from which the world should note
22 Something particular. His coin, ships, legions
May be a coward's, whose ministers would prevail
Under the service of a child as soon
As i' th' command of Caesar. I dare him therefore
26 To lay his gay comparisons apart
27 And answer me declined, sword against sword,
Ourselves alone. I'll write it : follow me.

[Exeunt Antony and Ambassador.]

---

8 *nicked* got the better of   10 *merèd question* sole cause (?), decisive factor
(?)   11 *course* chase   22 *Something particular* i.e. some personal heroism
26 *comparisons* i.e. all things which give him the advantage when he
compares his position with mine   27 *declined* i.e. in years and fortune

ENOBARBUS *[aside]*
    Yes, like enough : high-battled Caesar will   29
    Unstate his happiness and be staged to th' show   30
    Against a sworder ! I see men's judgments are
    A parcel of their fortunes, and things outward   32
    Do draw the inward quality after them   33
    To suffer all alike. That he should dream,   34
    Knowing all measures, the full Caesar will   35
    Answer his emptiness ! Caesar, thou has subdued
    His judgment too.
        Enter a Servant.
SERVANT   A messenger from Caesar.
CLEOPATRA
    What, no more ceremony ? See, my women,
    Against the blown rose may they stop their nose
    That kneeled unto the buds. Admit him, sir.
                [Exit Servant.]

ENOBARBUS *[aside]*
    Mine honesty and I begin to square.   41
    The loyalty well held to fools does make
    Our faith mere folly : yet he that can endure
    To follow with allegiance a fall'n lord
    Does conquer him that did his master conquer
    And earns a place i' th' story.
        Enter Thidias.
CLEOPATRA   Caesar's will ?
THIDIAS
    Hear it apart.
CLEOPATRA   None but friends : say boldly.
THIDIAS
    So, haply, are they friends to Antony.   48

---

29 *high-battled* lifted high in strength and mood by successful armies
30 *Unstate* abdicate   **30–31** *be . . . sworder* be exposed as a public spectacle
in a gladiatorial duel   **32** *A parcel* i.e. part and parcel   **33** *quality* nature
34 *To . . . alike* so that both decline together   **35** *Knowing all measures*
being a good judge (of men and things)   **41** *square* quarrel   **48** *haply*
most likely

ENOBARBUS
He needs as many, sir, as Caesar has,
Or needs not us. If Caesar please, our master
Will leap to be his friend; for us, you know,
52   Whose he is we are, and that is Caesar's.

THIDIAS   So.
Thus then, thou most renowned, Caesar entreats
54   Not to consider in what case thou stand'st
Further than he is Caesar.

CLEOPATRA   Go on: right royal.

THIDIAS
He knows that you embrace not Antony
As you did love, but as you feared him.

CLEOPATRA   O!

THIDIAS
The scars upon your honor therefore he
Does pity, as constrainèd blemishes,
Not as deserved.

CLEOPATRA   He is a god, and knows
What is most right. Mine honor was not yielded,
But conquered merely.

ENOBARBUS [aside]   To be sure of that,
I will ask Antony. Sir, sir, thou art so leaky
That we must leave thee to thy sinking, for
Thy dearest quit thee.   Exit Enobarbus.

THIDIAS   Shall I say to Caesar
66   What you require of him? For he partly begs
To be desired to give. It much would please him
That of his fortunes you should make a staff
To lean upon. But it would warm his spirits
To hear from me you had left Antony,
71   And put yourself under his shroud,
The universal landlord.

52 *Whose . . . are* i.e. whomever Antony belongs to, we belong to (?)
54–55 *Not . . . Caesar* i.e. not to think about your situation beyond realizing
that you have to do with (a generous conqueror like) Caesar   66 *require*
request   71 *shroud* shelter

CLEOPATRA   What's your name?
THIDIAS
  My name is Thidias.
CLEOPATRA   Most kind messenger,
  Say to great Caesar this: in deputation   74
  I kiss his conqu'ring hand; tell him I am prompt
  To lay my crown at's feet, and there to kneel.
  Tell him, from his all-obeying breath, I hear   77
  The doom of Egypt.
THIDIAS   'Tis your noblest course:
  Wisdom and fortune combating together,
  If that the former dare but what it can,   80
  No chance may shake it. Give me grace to lay
  My duty on your hand.   82
CLEOPATRA   Your Caesar's father oft,
  When he hath mused of taking kingdoms in,
  Bestowed his lips on that unworthy place,
  As it rained kisses.
     Enter Antony and Enobarbus.
ANTONY   Favors? by Jove that thunders!
  What art thou, fellow?
THIDIAS   One that but performs
  The bidding of the fullest man, and worthiest
  To have command obeyed.
ENOBARBUS *[aside]*   You will be whipped.
ANTONY
  Approach there! Ah, you kite! Now, gods and devils!
  Authority melts from me. Of late, when I cried 'Ho!'
  Like boys unto a muss, kings would start forth,   91
  And cry 'Your will?' Have you no ears? I am
  Antony yet.
     Enter a Servant.
           Take hence this Jack and whip him.   93

---

74 *in deputation* i.e. through you as deputy **77** *all-obeying* that all obey
80 *If . . . can* if discretion confines itself to the possible **82** *My duty* i.e.
a kiss **91** *muss* scramble **93** *Jack* conceited upstart

ENOBARBUS [aside]
 'Tis better playing with a lion's whelp
 Than with an old one dying.
ANTONY   Moon and stars!
 Whip him. Were't twenty of the greatest tributaries
 That do acknowledge Caesar, should I find them
98 So saucy with the hand of she here – what's her name
 Since she was Cleopatra? Whip him, fellows,
 Till like a boy you see him cringe his face
 And whine aloud for mercy. Take him hence.
THIDIAS
 Mark Antony –
ANTONY   Tug him away. Being whipped,
 Bring him again. This Jack of Caesar's shall
 Bear us an errand to him. *Exeunt [Servants] with Thidias.*
 You were half blasted ere I knew you. Ha!
 Have I my pillow left unpressed in Rome,
 Forborne the getting of a lawful race,
108 And by a gem of women, to be abused
109 By one that looks on feeders?
CLEOPATRA   Good my lord –
ANTONY
110 You have been a boggler ever:
 But when we in our viciousness grow hard
112 (O misery on't!) the wise gods seel our eyes,
 In our own filth drop our clear judgments, make us
 Adore our errors, laugh at's while we strut
 To our confusion.
CLEOPATRA   O, is't come to this?
ANTONY
 I found you as a morsel cold upon
117 Dead Caesar's trencher: nay, you were a fragment
 Of Gneius Pompey's, besides what hotter hours,

98–99 *what's . . . Cleopatra* (Antony implies that this common trafficker in kisses cannot be the imperial Cleopatra) 108 *abused* betrayed 109 *feeders* menials 110 *boggler* shifty one 112 *seel* sew up 117 *trencher* plate; *fragment* leftover

Unregist'red in vulgar fame, you have   119
Luxuriously picked out. For I am sure,   120
Though you can guess what temperance should be,
You know not what it is.

CLEOPATRA   Wherefore is this?

ANTONY
To let a fellow that will take rewards
And say 'God quit you!' be familiar with   124
My playfellow, your hand, this kingly seal
And plighter of high hearts. O that I were   126
Upon the hill of Basan to outroar
The hornèd herd! for I have savage cause,
And to proclaim it civilly were like   129
A haltered neck which does the hangman thank
For being yare about him.   131
    Enter a Servant with Thidias.
                Is he whipped?

SERVANT
Soundly, my lord.

ANTONY   Cried he? and begged 'a pardon?

SERVANT
He did ask favor.

ANTONY
If that thy father live, let him repent
Thou wast not made his daughter; and be thou sorry
To follow Caesar in his triumph, since
Thou hast been whipped for following him. Henceforth
The white hand of a lady fever thee,
Shake thou to look on't. Get thee back to Caesar,
Tell him thy entertainment: look thou say   140
He makes me angry with him. For he seems
Proud and disdainful, harping on what I am,

---

119 *vulgar fame* common gossip 120 *Luxuriously* lustfully 124 *quit*
repay 126–28 *O . . . herd* (Antony thinks of himself as chief among the
herd of bulls of Bashan whose roaring is described in Psalms xxii, 12–13 –
i.e. as chief cuckold among all the lovers cuckolded by Cleopatra) 129 *like*
to act like 131 *yare* nimble 140 *entertainment* reception (here)

Not what he knew I was. He makes me angry,
And at this time most easy 'tis to do't,
When my good stars that were my former guides
146 Have empty left their orbs and shot their fires
Into th' abysm of hell. If he mislike
My speech and what is done, tell him he has
149 Hipparchus, my enfranchèd bondman, whom
He may at pleasure whip, or hang, or torture,
As he shall like, to quit me. Urge it thou.
Hence with thy stripes, be gone!   *Exit Thidias.*

CLEOPATRA
Have you done yet?
153 ANTONY   Alack, our terrene moon
Is now eclipsed, and it portends alone
The fall of Antony.
155 CLEOPATRA   I must stay his time.
ANTONY
To flatter Caesar, would you mingle eyes
157 With one that ties his points?
CLEOPATRA   Not know me yet?
ANTONY
Cold-hearted toward me?
CLEOPATRA   Ah, dear, if I be so,
From my cold heart let heaven engender hail,
And poison it in the source, and the first stone
161 Drop in my neck: as it determines, so
Dissolve my life! The next Caesarion smite,
163 Till by degrees the memory of my womb,
Together with my brave Egyptians all,
165 By the discandying of this pelleted storm,
Lie graveless, till the flies and gnats of Nile
Have buried them for prey!

---

146 *orbs* the spheres in which they turn   149 *Hipparchus* (who had earlier
revolted to Caesar); *enfranchèd* freed   153 *our . . . moon* i.e. Cleopatra, our
terrestrial Isis or moon-goddess   155 *stay his time* wait out his fury   157
one . . . points his valet   161 *determines* melts   163 *the memory . . . womb*
i.e. my offspring   165 *discandying* melting (as if it were hard candy)

ANTONY   I am satisfied.
Caesar sits down in Alexandria, where
I will oppose his fate. Our force by land
Hath nobly held; our severed navy too
Have knit again, and fleet, threat'ning most sea-like.   171
Where hast thou been, my heart? Dost thou hear, lady?   172
If from the field I shall return once more
To kiss these lips, I will appear in blood;   174
I and my sword will earn our chronicle.   175
There's hope in't yet.

CLEOPATRA
That's my brave lord!

ANTONY
I will be treble-sinewed, hearted, breathed,
And fight maliciously; for when mine hours
Were nice and lucky, men did ransom lives   180
Of me for jests; but now I'll set my teeth
And send to darkness all that stop me. Come,
Let's have one other gaudy night: call to me   183
All my sad captains; fill our bowls once more;
Let's mock the midnight bell.

CLEOPATRA   It is my birthday.
I had thought t' have held it poor. But since my lord
Is Antony again, I will be Cleopatra.

ANTONY
We will yet do well.

CLEOPATRA
Call all his noble captains to my lord.

ANTONY
Do so, we'll speak to them; and to-night I'll force
The wine peep through their scars. Come on, my queen,
There's sap in't yet! The next time I do fight,   192
I'll make death love me, for I will contend
Even with his pestilent scythe. *Exeunt [all but Enobarbus].*

171 *fleet* are afloat   172 *heart* courage   174 *in blood* (1) bloody, (2) with
blood up, spirited   175 *our chronicle* our place in history   180 *nice* able
to be 'choosy'   183 *gaudy* joyous   192 *sap* i.e. life, hope

ENOBARBUS
Now he'll outstare the lightning. To be furious
Is to be frighted out of fear, and in that mood
197   The dove will peck the estridge ; and I see still
A diminution in our captain's brain
Restores his heart. When valor preys on reason,
It eats the sword it fights with : I will seek
Some way to leave him.   *Exit.*

*

IV, i   *Enter Caesar, Agrippa, and Maecenas, with his
Army, Caesar reading a letter.*

CAESAR
He calls me boy, and chides as he had power
To beat me out of Egypt. My messenger
He hath whipped with rods ; dares me to personal combat,
Caesar to Antony. Let the old ruffian know
I have many other ways to die, meantime
Laugh at his challenge.
MAECENAS   Caesar must think,
When one so great begins to rage, he's hunted
Even to falling. Give him no breath, but now
9   Make boot of his distraction : never anger
Made good guard for itself.
CAESAR   Let our best heads
Know that to-morrow the last of many battles
12   We mean to fight. Within our files there are,
Of those that served Mark Antony but late,
14   Enough to fetch him in. See it done,
And feast the army ; we have store to do't,
And they have earned the waste. Poor Antony ! *Exeunt.*

*

197 *estridge* species of hawk
IV, i The camp of Octavius Caesar   9 *boot* advantage   12 *files* troops
14 *fetch him in* capture him

Enter Antony, Cleopatra, Enobarbus, Charmian,   IV, ii
Iras, Alexas, with others.

ANTONY
He will not fight with me, Domitius?

ENOBARBUS   No.

ANTONY
Why should he not?

ENOBARBUS
He thinks, being twenty times of better fortune,
He is twenty men to one.

ANTONY   To-morrow, soldier,
By sea and land I'll fight: or I will live,   5
Or bathe my dying honor in the blood
Shall make it live again. Woo't thou fight well?

ENOBARBUS
I'll strike, and cry 'Take all!'   8

ANTONY   Well said, come on;
Call forth my household servants; let's to-night
Be bounteous at our meal.

Enter three or four Servitors.

                      Give me thy hand,
Thou hast been rightly honest, so hast thou,
And thou, and thou, and thou: you have served me well,
And kings have been your fellows.

CLEOPATRA   What means this?   13

ENOBARBUS
'Tis one of those odd tricks which sorrow shoots
Out of the mind.

ANTONY   And thou art honest too.
I wish I could be made so many men,   16
And all of you clapped up together in
An Antony, that I might do you service
So good as you have done.

OMNES   The gods forbid!

IV, ii The palace of Cleopatra   **5** *or* either   **8** *Take all* winner take all
13–15 (here and in ll. 23–24 Enobarbus and Cleopatra talk aside)   **16** *so
many men* i.e. so many men as you are

ANTONY
Well, my good fellows, wait on me to-night:
Scant not my cups, and make as much of me
As when mine empire was your fellow too
And suffered my command.
CLEOPATRA   What does he mean?
ENOBARBUS
To make his followers weep.
ANTONY   Tend me to-night;
25 May be it is the period of your duty.
26 Haply you shall not see me more; or if,
A mangled shadow. Perchance to-morrow
You'll serve another master. I look on you
As one that takes his leave. Mine honest friends,
I turn you not away, but like a master
Married to your good service, stay till death.
Tend me to-night two hours, I ask no more,
33 And the gods yield you for't!
ENOBARBUS   What mean you, sir,
To give them this discomfort? Look, they weep,
And I, an ass, am onion-eyed; for shame!
Transform us not to women.
ANTONY   Ho, ho, ho!
Now the witch take me if I meant it thus!
38 Grace grow where those drops fall! My hearty friends,
You take me in too dolorous a sense,
For I spake to you for your comfort, did desire you
To burn this night with torches. Know, my hearts,
I hope well of to-morrow, and will lead you
Where rather I'll expect victorious life
Than death and honor. Let's to supper, come,
And drown consideration.   *Exeunt.*

*

25 *period* end   26 *Haply* most likely   33 *yield* repay   38 *Grace grow* may
virtues spring up (with a pun on 'grace' as one name for the herb rue)

Enter a Company of Soldiers. IV, iii

1. SOLDIER
Brother, good night : to-morrow is the day.

2. SOLDIER
It will determine one way : fare you well.
Heard you of nothing strange about the streets ?

1. SOLDIER
Nothing. What news ?

2. SOLDIER
Belike 'tis but a rumor. Good night to you.

1. SOLDIER
Well, sir, good night.
They meet other Soldiers.

2. SOLDIER   Soldiers, have careful watch.

3. SOLDIER
And you. Good night, good night.
They place themselves in every corner of the stage.

4. SOLDIER
Here we; and if to-morrow   8
Our navy thrive, I have an absolute hope
Our landmen will stand up.

3. SOLDIER   'Tis a brave army,
And full of purpose.
Music of the hautboys is under the stage.

2. SOLDIER   Peace! What noise ?

1. SOLDIER   List, list !

2. SOLDIER
Hark !

1. SOLDIER Music i' th' air.

3. SOLDIER   Under the earth.

4. SOLDIER
It signs well, does it not ?   13

3. SOLDIER   No.

1. SOLDIER   Peace, I say !
What should this mean ?

IV, iii An open place in Alexandria   8 *Here we* i.e. here is our post   13
signs signifies

2 . SOLDIER

15   'Tis the god Hercules, whom Antony loved,
Now leaves him.

1 . SOLDIER   Walk; let's see if other watchmen
Do hear what we do.

2 . SOLDIER   How now, masters?

OMNES *(speak together)*   How now?
How now? Do you hear this?

1 . SOLDIER   Ay. Is't not strange?

3 . SOLDIER
Do you hear, masters? do you hear?

1 . SOLDIER

20   Follow the noise so far as we have quarter.
Let's see how it will give off.

OMNES
Content. 'Tis strange.   *Exeunt.*

*

IV, iv   *Enter Antony and Cleopatra, with others.*

ANTONY
Eros! mine armor, Eros!

CLEOPATRA   Sleep a little.

ANTONY
No, my chuck. Eros, come; mine armor, Eros.
Enter Eros [with armor].

3   Come, good fellow, put thine iron on.
If fortune be not ours to-day, it is
Because we brave her. Come.

CLEOPATRA   Nay, I'll help too.
What's this for?

ANTONY   Ah, let be, let be! Thou art

7   The armorer of my heart. False, false; this, this.

CLEOPATRA
Sooth, la, I'll help: thus it must be.

---

15 *Hercules* (cf. I, iii, 84–85n.)   **20** *as . . . quarter* as our watch extends
IV, iv The palace of Cleopatra   **3** *thine iron* i.e. this armor of mine   **7**
False wrong

ANTONY   Well, well,
We shall thrive now. Seest thou, my good fellow?
Go, put on thy defenses.
EROS   Briefly, sir.   10
CLEOPATRA
Is not this buckled well?
ANTONY   Rarely, rarely:
He that unbuckles this, till we do please
To daff't for our repose, shall hear a storm.   13
Thou fumblest, Eros, and my queen's a squire
More tight at this than thou. Dispatch. O love,   15
That thou couldst see my wars to-day, and knew'st
The royal occupation: thou shouldst see
A workman in't.   18
         Enter an armed Soldier.
                          Good morrow to thee, welcome,
Thou look'st like him that knows a warlike charge.   19
To business that we love we rise betime   20
And go to't with delight.
SOLDIER   A thousand, sir,
Early though't be, have on their riveted trim,   22
And at the port expect you.   23
         Shout. Trumpets flourish. Enter Captains and
         Soldiers.
CAPTAIN
The morn is fair. Good morrow, General.
ALL
Good morrow, General.
ANTONY   'Tis well blown, lads.   25
This morning, like the spirit of a youth
That means to be of note, begins betimes.
So, so. Come, give me that: this way. Well said.   28
Fare thee well, dame; whate'er becomes of me,

10 *Briefly* in a moment   13 *daff't* take it off   15 *tight* deft   18 *workman*
craftsman, expert   19 *charge* duty   20 *betime* early   22 *riveted trim* armor
23 *port* gate   25 *blown* opened (i.e. the morning)   28 *said* done (spoken to
Cleopatra, who is arming him)

This is a soldier's kiss. Rebukable
31   And worthy shameful check it were to stand
On more mechanic compliment. I'll leave thee
Now like a man of steel. You that will fight,
Follow me close; I'll bring you to't. Adieu.
                    Exeunt [Antony, Eros, Captains, and Soldiers].

CHARMIAN
Please you retire to your chamber?

CLEOPATRA   Lead me.
He goes forth gallantly. That he and Caesar might
Determine this great war in single fight!
Then Antony – but now – Well, on.   *Exeunt.*

*

IV, v   *Trumpets sound. Enter Antony and Eros [, a Soldier*
                meeting them].

SOLDIER
The gods make this a happy day to Antony!

ANTONY
Would thou and those thy scars had once prevailed
To make me fight at land!

SOLDIER   Hadst thou done so,
The kings that have revolted and the soldier
That has this morning left thee would have still
Followèd thy heels.

ANTONY   Who's gone this morning?

SOLDIER   Who?
One ever near thee: call for Enobarbus,
He shall not hear thee, or from Caesar's camp
Say 'I am none of thine.'

ANTONY   What sayest thou?

SOLDIER   Sir,
He is with Caesar.

31 *check* reproof   31–32 *stand . . . compliment* use more elaborate ceremony
IV, v An open place in Alexandria

120

EROS   Sir, his chests and treasure
  He has not with him.
ANTONY   Is he gone?
SOLDIER   Most certain.
ANTONY
  Go, Eros, send his treasure after; do it;
  Detain no jot, I charge thee. Write to him
  (I will subscribe) gentle adieus and greetings;   14
  Say that I wish he never find more cause
  To change a master. O, my fortunes have
  Corrupted honest men! Dispatch. Enobarbus!
                    Exit [with Eros and Soldier].

                    *

        Flourish. Enter Agrippa, Caesar, with Enobarbus, IV, vi
        and Dolabella.
CAESAR
  Go forth, Agrippa, and begin the fight.
  Our will is Antony be took alive:
  Make it so known.
AGRIPPA
  Caesar, I shall.   *[Exit.]*
CAESAR
  The time of universal peace is near.
  Prove this a prosp'rous day, the three-nooked world   6
  Shall bear the olive freely.
        Enter a Messenger.
MESSENGER   Antony
  Is come into the field.
CAESAR   Go charge Agrippa
  Plant those that have revolted in the vant,   9
  That Antony may seem to spend his fury
  Upon himself.   *Exeunt [all but Enobarbus].* 11

---

14 *subscribe* sign
IV, vi The camp of Octavius Caesar **6** *three-nooked* three-cornered
(Africa, Asia, Europe) **9** *vant* front lines **11** *himself* i.e. his own former
soldiers

ENOBARBUS
Alexas did revolt and went to Jewry on
13 Affairs of Antony; there did dissuade
Great Herod to incline himself to Caesar
And leave his master Antony. For this pains
Caesar hath hanged him. Canidius and the rest
17 That fell away have entertainment, but
No honorable trust. I have done ill,
Of which I do accuse myself so sorely
That I will joy no more.

Enter a Soldier of Caesar's.

SOLDIER   Enobarbus, Antony
Hath after thee sent all thy treasure, with
His bounty overplus. The messenger
Came on my guard, and at thy tent is now
Unloading of his mules.

ENOBARBUS   I give it you.

SOLDIER
Mock not, Enobarbus.
26 I tell you true. Best you safed the bringer
Out of the host; I must attend mine office
Or would have done't myself. Your emperor
Continues still a Jove.   *Exit.*

ENOBARBUS
I am alone the villain of the earth,
And feel I am so most. O Antony,
Thou mine of bounty, how wouldst thou have paid
My better service, when my turpitude
34 Thou dost so crown with gold! This blows my heart.
35 If swift thought break it not, a swifter mean
Shall outstrike thought; but thought will do't, I feel.
I fight against thee? No, I will go seek
Some ditch wherein to die: the foul'st best fits
My latter part of life.   *Exit.*

*

13 *dissuade* i.e. from Antony   17 *entertainment* employment   26 *safed* gave
safe conduct to   34 *blows* makes well   35 *thought* grief

Alarum. Drums and Trumpets. Enter Agrippa   IV, vii
[and Soldiers].

AGRIPPA
Retire. We have engaged ourselves too far.   1
Caesar himself has work, and our oppression   2
Exceeds what we expected.   *Exit [with Soldiers].*
    Alarums. Enter Antony, and Scarus wounded.

SCARUS
O my brave Emperor, this is fought indeed!
Had we done so at first, we had droven them home
With clouts about their heads.   6
ANTONY   Thou bleed'st apace.

SCARUS
I had a wound here that was like a T,
But now 'tis made an H.   8
    [Sound retreat] far off.
ANTONY   They do retire.

SCARUS
We'll beat 'em into bench-holes. I have yet   9
Room for six scotches more.   10
    Enter Eros.

EROS
They are beaten, sir, and our advantage serves
For a fair victory.
SCARUS   Let us score their backs   12
And snatch 'em up, as we take hares, behind:
'Tis sport to maul a runner.
ANTONY   I will reward thee
Once for thy sprightly comfort, and tenfold
For thy good valor. Come thee on.
SCARUS   I'll halt after.   16
    Exeunt.

IV, vii A field near Alexandria **1** *engaged* entangled (with the enemy)
2 *our oppression* the pressure on us **6** *clouts* bandages **3** *H* (pun on
'ache,' which was pronounced 'aitch') **9** *bench-holes* privy holes **10**
scotches gashes **12** *score* mark **16** *halt* limp

IV, viii   *Alarum. Enter Antony again in a march ; Scarus,*
                 with others.

ANTONY
    We have beat him to his camp. Run one before
2   And let the Queen know of our gests. To-morrow,
    Before the sun shall see 's, we'll spill the blood
    That has to-day escaped. I thank you all,
    For doughty-handed are you, and have fought
    Not as you served the cause, but as 't had been
7   Each man's like mine : you have shown all Hectors.
8   Enter the city, clip your wives, your friends,
    Tell them your feats, whilst they with joyful tears
    Wash the congealment from your wounds, and kiss
    The honored gashes whole.
         Enter Cleopatra.
         [To Scarus]   Give me thy hand ;
12   To this great fairy I'll commend thy acts,
    Make her thanks bless thee. – O thou day o' th' world,
    Chain mine armed neck ; leap thou, attire and all,
15   Through proof of harness to my heart, and there
16   Ride on the pants triumphing.
    CLEOPATRA   Lord of lords !
17   O infinite virtue, com'st thou smiling from
18   The world's great snare uncaught ?
    ANTONY   My nightingale,
    We have beat them to their beds. What, girl ! though
       gray
    Do something mingle with our younger brown, yet ha'
       we
    A brain that nourishes our nerves, and can
22   Get goal for goal of youth. Behold this man :
    Commend unto his lips thy favoring hand. –

IV, viii Before the gates of Alexandria **2** *gests* deeds **7** *shown* proved
8 *clip* hug **12** *fairy* enchantress **15** *proof of harness* i.e. impenetrable
armor **16** *Ride . . . pants* i.e. as if his heart were a panting steed **17**
virtue valor **18** *snare* i.e. death in war **22** *Get . . . of* hold our own with

Kiss it, my warrior. – He hath fought to-day
As if a god in hate of mankind had
Destroyed in such a shape.
CLEOPATRA   I'll give thee, friend,
An armor all of gold ; it was a king's.
ANTONY
He has deserved it, were it carbuncled   28
Like holy Phoebus' car. Give me thy hand.   29
Through Alexandria make a jolly march ;
Bear our hacked targets like the men that owe them.   31
Had our great palace the capacity
To camp this host, we all would sup together
And drink carouses to the next day's fate,
Which promises royal peril. Trumpeters,
With brazen din blast you the city's ear,
Make mingle with our rattling tabourines,
That heaven and earth may strike their sounds together,
Applauding our approach.   *Exeunt*.

*

Enter a Sentry and his Company. Enobarbus   IV, ix
    follows.
SENTRY
If we be not relieved within this hour,
We must return to th' court of guard. The night
Is shiny, and they say we shall embattle
By th' second hour i' th' morn.
1 . WATCHMAN   This last day was
A shrewd one to's.   5
ENOBARBUS   O, bear me witness, night –
2 . WATCHMAN
What man is this ?
1 . WATCHMAN   Stand close, and list him.

28 *carbuncled* jewelled   29 *holy Phoebus' car* the sun-god's chariot   31
targets shields; *owe* own
IV, ix The camp of Octavius Caesar   5 *shrewd* wicked

125

ENOBARBUS
    Be witness to me, O thou blessèd moon,
8   When men revolted shall upon record
    Bear hateful memory, poor Enobarbus did
    Before thy face repent!
SENTRY   Enobarbus?
2. WATCHMAN   Peace:
    Hark further.
ENOBARBUS
12   O sovereign mistress of true melancholy,
13   The poisonous damp of night disponge upon me,
    That life, a very rebel to my will,
    May hang no longer on me. Throw my heart
    Against the flint and hardness of my fault,
17   Which, being dried with grief, will break to powder,
    And finish all foul thoughts. O Antony,
    Nobler than my revolt is infamous,
20   Forgive me in thine own particular,
21   But let the world rank me in register
22   A master leaver and a fugitive.
    O Antony! O Antony!
        [Dies.]
1. WATCHMAN   Let's speak
To him.
SENTRY Let's hear him, for the things he speaks
May concern Caesar.
2. WATCHMAN   Let's do so. But he sleeps.
SENTRY
26   Swoonds rather, for so bad a prayer as his
27   Was never yet for sleep.
1. WATCHMAN   Go we to him.

8–9 *When ... memory* when traitors go down in history shamed **12** *mistress*
i.e. the moon **13** *disponge* squeeze (as from a sponge) **17** *Which* (refers
to *heart*); *dried* (sorrow was thought to dry up the blood) **20** *in ... particular*
i.e. yourself **21** *in register* in its records **22** *master leaver* (1) runaway
servant, (2) outstanding traitor **26** *Swoonds* faints **27** *for sleep* conducive
to sleep

2. WATCHMAN
Awake, sir, awake, speak to us.

1. WATCHMAN   Hear you, sir?

SENTRY
The hand of death hath raught him.   29
          Drums afar off.   Hark! The drums
Demurely wake the sleepers. Let us bear him   30
To th' court of guard: he is of note. Our hour
Is fully out.

2. WATCHMAN
Come on then,
He may recover yet.   *Exeunt [with the body].*

*

          Enter Antony and Scarus, with their Army.   IV, x

ANTONY
Their preparation is to-day by sea;
We please them not by land.

SCARUS   For both, my lord.

ANTONY
I would they'ld fight i' th' fire or i' th' air;
We'ld fight there too. But this it is, our foot
Upon the hills adjoining to the city   4
Shall stay with us – Order for sea is given;
They have put forth the haven –
Where their appointment we may best discover   8
And look on their endeavor.   *Exeunt.*

          Enter Caesar and his Army.   IV, xi

CAESAR
But being charged, we will be still by land,   1
Which, as I take't, we shall; for his best force
Is forth to man his galleys. To the vales,
And hold our best advantage.   *Exeunt.*

---

29 *raught* reached   **30** *Demurely* softly
IV, x A field near Alexandria   **4** *foot* infantry   **8** *appointment* arrangement
IV, xi   **1** *But being* unless we are

IV, xii   *Enter Antony and Scarus.*

ANTONY

> Yet they are not joined. Where yond pine does stand
> I shall discover all. I'll bring thee word
> Straight how 'tis like to go.   *Exit.*

SCARUS   Swallows have built
> In Cleopatra's sails their nests. The augurers
> Say they know not, they cannot tell, look grimly,
> And dare not speak their knowledge. Antony
> Is valiant, and dejected, and by starts

8   His fretted fortunes give him hope and fear
> Of what he has, and has not.

> > *Alarum afar off, as at a sea-fight.*
> > *Enter Antony.*

ANTONY   All is lost !
> This foul Egyptian hath betrayed me :
> My fleet hath yielded to the foe, and yonder
> They cast their caps up and carouse together

13   Like friends long lost. Triple-turned whore ! 'tis thou
> Hast sold me to this novice, and my heart
> Makes only wars on thee. Bid them all fly ;

16   For when I am revenged upon my charm,
> I have done all. Bid them all fly, be gone.   *[Exit Scarus.]*
> O sun, thy uprise shall I see no more.
> Fortune and Antony part here, even here
> Do we shake hands. All come to this ? The hearts
> That spanieled me at heels, to whom I gave

22   Their wishes, do discandy, melt their sweets
23   On blossoming Caesar ; and this pine is barked,
> That overtopped them all. Betrayed I am.
25   O this false soul of Egypt ! this grave charm,
> Whose eye becked forth my wars, and called them home,
27   Whose bosom was my crownet, my chief end,

IV, xii   **8** *fretted* shifting   **13** *Triple-turned* i.e. from Pompey, from Julius
Caesar, and now from himself   **16** *charm* enchantress   **22** *discandy* melt
23 *barked* stripped   **25** *grave* deadly   **27** *my crownet . . . end* the crown and
purpose of my life

Like a right gypsy hath at fast and loose   28
Beguiled me to the very heart of loss.
What, Eros, Eros!

    Enter Cleopatra.

                  Ah, thou spell! Avaunt!   30

CLEOPATRA
Why is my lord enraged against his love?

ANTONY
Vanish, or I shall give thee thy deserving
And blemish Caesar's triumph. Let him take thee   33
And hoist thee up to the shouting plebeians;
Follow his chariot, like the greatest spot
Of all thy sex. Most monster-like be shown
For poor'st diminitives, for dolts, and let   37
Patient Octavia plough thy visage up
With her preparèd nails.   *Exit Cleopatra.*
              'Tis well th' art gone,
If it be well to live; but better 'twere
Thou fell'st into my fury, for one death
Might have prevented many. Eros, ho!
The shirt of Nessus is upon me; teach me,   43
Alcides, thou mine ancestor, thy rage.   44
Let me lodge Lichas on the horns o' th' moon
And with those hands that grasped the heaviest club
Subdue my worthiest self. The witch shall die.
To the young Roman boy she hath sold me, and I fall
Under this plot: she dies for't. Eros, ho!   *Exit.*

                     *

---

28 *right* true; *fast and loose* (a game)   **30** *Avaunt* be gone   **33** *triumph* triumphal procession (in Rome)   **37** *diminitives* little people, i.e. the populace   **43** *Nessus* (Fatally wounded by Hercules with a poisoned arrow, the centaur Nessus persuaded Hercules' wife to give his blood-stained shirt to her husband, telling her it would assure his love for her. The shirt so poisoned Hercules that in his agony he threw his page Lichas, who had brought it, to the skies and set about destroying himself.)   **44** *Alcides* Hercules

IV, xiii   *Enter Cleopatra, Charmian, Iras, Mardian.*

CLEOPATRA
Help me, my women : O, he's more mad
2   Than Telamon for his shield ; the boar of Thessaly
3   Was never so embossed.

CHARMIAN   To th' monument !
There lock yourself, and send him word you are dead.
5   The soul and body rive not more in parting
Than greatness going off.

CLEOPATRA   To th' monument !
Mardian, go tell him I have slain myself :
Say that the last I spoke was 'Antony'
And word it, prithee, piteously. Hence, Mardian,
And bring me how he takes my death. To th' monument !
                                              Exeunt.

*

IV, xiv   *Enter Antony and Eros.*

ANTONY
Eros, thou yet behold'st me ?

EROS   Ay, noble lord.

ANTONY
Sometime we see a cloud that's dragonish ;
A vapor sometime like a bear or lion,
A towered citadel, a pendant rock,
A forkèd mountain, or blue promontory
With trees upon't that nod unto the world
And mock our eyes with air. Thou hast seen these signs ;
8   They are black Vesper's pageants.

EROS   Ay, my lord.

IV, xiii The palace of Cleopatra 2 *Telamon* Ajax Telamon, who went mad
when Achilles' shield was not given to him but to his rival, Ulysses; *boar of
Thessaly* (sent by Artemis to ravage Thessaly in punishment for omitted
sacrifices) 3 *embossed* infuriated; *monument* tomb (which like other
Egyptian rulers Cleopatra had prepared in advance) 5 *rive* rend
IV, xiv Near the palace of Cleopatra 8 *black Vesper's pageants* i.e. shows
heralding the coming of night (as pageants used to herald the coming of
a king or queen)

ANTONY

>That which is now a horse, even with a thought
>The rack dislimns, and makes it indistinct   10
>As water is in water.

EROS   It does, my lord.

ANTONY

>My good knave Eros, now thy captain is
>Even such a body: here I am Antony,
>Yet cannot hold this visible shape, my knave.
>I made these wars for Egypt, and the Queen,   15
>Whose heart I thought I had, for she had mine,
>Which, whilst it was mine, had annexed unto't
>A million moe, now lost – she, Eros, has   18
>Packed cards with Caesar, and false-played my glory   19
>Unto an enemy's triumph.   20
>Nay, weep not, gentle Eros, there is left us
>Ourselves to end ourselves.
>>   *Enter Mardian.*   O, thy vile lady!
>She has robbed me of my sword.   23

MARDIAN   No, Antony.

>My mistress loved thee and her fortunes mingled
>With thine entirely.

ANTONY   Hence, saucy eunuch, peace!

>She hath betrayed me and shall die the death.

MARDIAN

>Death of one person can be paid but once,
>And that she has discharged. What thou wouldst do
>Is done unto thy hand. The last she spake
>Was 'Antony! most noble Antony!'
>Then in the midst a tearing groan did break
>The name of Antony; it was divided
>Between her heart and lips: she rend'red life,
>Thy name so buried in her.

---

10 *rack* cloud; *dislimns* unshapes   **15** *Egypt* i.e. Cleopatra   **18** *moe* more
19 *Packed* i.e. stacked the deck; *false-played* falsely played away   **20**
triumph (1) victory, (2) trump   **23** *sword* manhood and soldiership

ANTONY   Dead, then?
MARDIAN   Dead.
ANTONY
    Unarm, Eros. The long day's task is done, — *time to die*
    And we must sleep.
          [To Mardian] That thou depart'st hence safe
    Does pay thy labor richly: go.   *Exit Mardian.*
                    Off, pluck off:

38   The sevenfold shield of Ajax cannot keep
39   The battery from my heart. O, cleave, my sides!
40   Heart, once be stronger than thy continent,
      Crack thy frail case! Apace, Eros, apace.
      No more a soldier. Bruisèd pieces, go;
      You have been nobly borne. – From me awhile. *Exit Eros.*
      I will o'ertake thee, Cleopatra, and
      Weep for my pardon. So it must be, for now
46   All length is torture: since the torch is out,
47   Lie down, and stray no farther. Now all labor
      Mars what it does; yea, very force entangles
49   Itself with strength: seal then, and all is done.
      Eros! – I come, my queen. – Eros! – Stay for me.
51   Where souls do couch on flowers, we'll hand in hand,
52   And with our sprightly port make the ghosts gaze:
53   Dido and her Aeneas shall want troops,
      And all the haunt be ours. – Come, Eros, Eros!
          Enter Eros.

Elysian fields

EROS
    What would my lord?
ANTONY   Since Cleopatra died
    I have lived in such dishonor that the gods

---

38 *sevenfold* having seven thicknesses   **39** *battery* the battering (of grief)
40 *continent* i.e. that which contains thee   **46** *length* i.e. of life   **47–49**
labor . . . strength i.e. force is defeated by its own strength, labor by its own
effort   **49** *seal* bring all to a close (as in sealing a document or will)   **51**
Where . . . flowers i.e. in the Elysian fields   **52** *port* behavior   **53** *want*
troops lack admirers (i.e. in comparison with us as faithful lovers – since
Aeneas deserted Dido for Roman greatness whereas Antony is deserting
Roman greatness for Cleopatra)

Detest my baseness. I, that with my sword
Quartered the world and o'er green Neptune's back
With ships made cities, condemn myself to lack   59
The courage of a woman – less noble mind
Than she which by her death our Caesar tells
'I am conqueror of myself.' Thou art sworn, Eros,
That, when the exigent should come, which now   63
Is come indeed, when I should see behind me
Th' inevitable prosecution of   65
Disgrace and horror, that on my command
Thou then wouldst kill me. Do't, the time is come.
Thou strik'st not me, 'tis Caesar thou defeat'st.
Put color in thy cheek.

EROS   The gods withhold me!
Shall I do that which all the Parthian darts,
Though enemy, lost aim and could not?

ANTONY   Eros,
Wouldst thou be windowed in great Rome and see   72
Thy master thus with pleached arms, bending down   73
His corrigible neck, his face subdued   74
To penetrative shame, whilst the wheeled seat   75
Of fortunate Caesar, drawn before him, branded
His baseness that ensued?   77

EROS   I would not see't.

ANTONY
Come then: for with a wound I must be cured.
Draw thou thy honest sword, which thou hast worn
Most useful for thy country.

EROS   O sir, pardon me.

ANTONY
When I did make thee free, swor'st thou not then
To do this when I bade thee? Do it at once,
Or thy precedent services are all   83

---

59 *to lack* for lacking **63** *exigent* need **65** *prosecution* pursuit **72** *windowed* i.e. watching from a window **73** *pleached* folded **74** *corrigible* submissive **75** *penetrative* penetrating **77** *His . . . ensued* the baseness of him that followed **83** *precedent* former

But accidents unpurposed. Draw, and come.

EROS

Turn from me then that noble countenance
Wherein the worship of the whole world lies.

ANTONY

Lo thee!
    [Turns from him.]

EROS

My sword is drawn.

ANTONY   Then let it do at once
The thing why thou hast drawn it.

EROS   My dear master,
My captain, and my emperor, let me say,
Before I strike this bloody stroke, farewell.

ANTONY

'Tis said, man, and farewell.

EROS

Farewell, great chief. Shall I strike now?

ANTONY   Now, Eros.

EROS

Why, there then! Thus I do escape the sorrow
Of Antony's death.
    Kills himself.

ANTONY   Thrice-nobler than myself!
Thou teachest me, O valiant Eros, what
I should, and thou couldst not. My queen and Eros
98   Have by their brave instruction got upon me
A nobleness in record. But I will be
A bridegroom in my death, and run into't
As to a lover's bed. Come then; and, Eros,
Thy master dies thy scholar. To do thus
    [Falls on his sword.]
I learned of thee. How? not dead? not dead?
The guard, ho! O, dispatch me!

98–99 *got ... record* beaten me to a noble name in history

134

Enter [Decretas and] a [Company of the] Guard.   104

1. GUARDSMAN   What's the noise?

ANTONY

I have done my work ill, friends. O, make an end
Of what I have begun.

2. GUARDSMAN   The star is fall'n.

1. GUARDSMAN

And time is at his period.   107

ALL   Alas, and woe!

ANTONY

Let him that loves me strike me dead.

1. GUARDSMAN

Not I.

2. GUARDSMAN   Nor I.

3. GUARDSMAN   Nor any one.

                    Exeunt [the Guardsmen].

DECRETAS

Thy death and fortunes bid thy followers fly.
This sword but shown to Caesar, with this tidings,
Shall enter me with him.   113

                    Enter Diomedes.

DIOMEDES

Where's Antony?

DECRETAS   There, Diomed, there.

DIOMEDES   Lives he?
Wilt thou not answer, man?   *[Exit Decretas.]*

ANTONY

Art thou there, Diomed? Draw thy sword, and give me
Sufficing strokes for death.

DIOMEDES   Most absolute lord,
My mistress Cleopatra sent me to thee.

ANTONY

When did she send thee?

---

104 s.d. *Decretas* (the usual folio spelling of a name which also appears in
the folio as 'Dercetus' and is sometimes revised by editors to 'Dercetas')
107 *period* end   **113** *enter* recommend

DIOMEDES   Now, my lord.

ANTONY   Where is she?

DIOMEDES

Locked in her monument. She had a prophesying fear
Of what hath come to pass; for when she saw
(Which never shall be found) you did suspect

123 She had disposed with Caesar, and that your rage

124 Would not be purged, she sent you word she was dead;
But, fearing since how it might work, hath sent
Me to proclaim the truth, and I am come,
I dread, too late.

ANTONY

Too late, good Diomed. Call my guard, I prithee.

DIOMEDES

What ho! the Emperor's guard! the guard, what ho!
Come, your lord calls!

       Enter four or five of the Guard of Antony.

ANTONY

Bear me, good friends, where Cleopatra bides;
'Tis the last service that I shall command you.

1. GUARDSMAN

Woe, woe are we, sir, you may not live to wear
All your true followers out.

ALL   Most heavy day!

ANTONY

Nay, good my fellows, do not please sharp fate
To grace it with your sorrows. Bid that welcome
Which comes to punish us, and we punish it,
Seeming to bear it lightly. Take me up:
I have led you oft; carry me now, good friends,
And have my thanks for all.

       Exit [the Guard,] bearing Antony.

*

123 *disposed* made terms   124 *purged* expelled

Enter Cleopatra and her Maids aloft, with   IV, xv
Charmian and Iras.

CLEOPATRA
O Charmian, I will never go from hence.

CHARMIAN
Be comforted, dear madam.

CLEOPATRA   No, I will not.
All strange and terrible events are welcome,
But comforts we despise. Our size of sorrow,
Proportioned to our cause, must be as great
As that which makes it.
    Enter Diomed [below].
            How now? Is he dead?

DIOMEDES
His death's upon him, but not dead.
Look out o' th' other side your monument;
His guard have brought him thither.
    Enter [below,] Antony, and the Guard [bearing
    him].

CLEOPATRA   O sun,
Burn the great sphere thou mov'st in, darkling stand   10
The varying shore o' th' world! O Antony,
Antony, Antony! Help, Charmian, help, Iras, help:
Help, friends below, let's draw him hither.

ANTONY   Peace!
Not Caesar's valor hath o'erthrown Antony,
But Antony's hath triumphed on itself.

CLEOPATRA
So it should be, that none but Antony
Should conquer Antony, but woe 'tis so!

ANTONY
I am dying, Egypt, dying; only
I here importune death awhile, until   19
Of many thousand kisses the poor last
I lay upon thy lips.

IV, xv Before the monument of Cleopatra   10 *darkling* darkened   19
importune beg to delay

21 CLEOPATRA   I dare not, dear ;
            Dear my lord, pardon : I dare not,
            Lest I be taken. Not th' imperious show
            Of the full-fortuned Caesar ever shall
25   Be brooched with me, if knife, drugs, serpents have
            Edge, sting, or operation. I am safe :
            Your wife Octavia, with her modest eyes
28   And still conclusion, shall acquire no honor
29   Demuring upon me. But come, come, Antony !
            Help me, my women, we must draw thee up :
            Assist, good friends.
        ANTONY   O, quick, or I am gone.
        CLEOPATRA
            Here's sport indeed ! How heavy weighs my lord !
33   Our strength is all gone into heaviness :
            That makes the weight. Had I great Juno's power,
            The strong-winged Mercury should fetch thee up
            And set thee by Jove's side. Yet come a little,
            Wishers were ever fools. O, come, come, come.
                They heave Antony aloft to Cleopatra.
            And welcome, welcome ! Die when thou hast lived,
39   Quicken with kissing. Had my lips that power,
            Thus would I wear them out.
        ALL   A heavy sight !
        ANTONY
            I am dying, Egypt, dying.
            Give me some wine, and let me speak a little.
        CLEOPATRA
            No, let me speak, and let me rail so high
44   That the false huswife Fortune break her wheel,
            Provoked by my offense.
        ANTONY   One word, sweet queen.
            Of Caesar seek your honor, with your safety. O !

---

21 *dare not* i.e. dare not descend to Antony's side   25 *brooched* adorned
28 *still conclusion* wordless censure   29 *Demuring* looking demurely
33 *heaviness* (with pun on 'grief')   39 *Quicken* come back to life   44
huswife jilt

CLEOPATRA
  They do not go together.
ANTONY   Gentle, hear me:
  None about Caesar trust but Proculeius.
CLEOPATRA
  My resolution and my hands I'll trust,
  None about Caesar.
ANTONY
  The miserable change now at my end
  Lament nor sorrow at; but please your thoughts
  In feeding them with those my former fortunes,
  Wherein I lived the greatest prince o' th' world,
  The noblest: and do now not basely die,
  Not cowardly put off my helmet to
  My countryman. A Roman, by a Roman
  Valiantly vanquished. Now my spirit is going,
  I can no more.
CLEOPATRA   Noblest of men, woo't die?   59
  Hast thou no care of me? Shall I abide
  In this dull world, which in thy absence is
  No better than a sty? O, see, my women,
      [Antony dies.]
  The crown o' th' earth doth melt. My lord!
  O, withered is the garland of the war,   64
  The soldier's pole is fall'n: young boys and girls   65
  Are level now with men. The odds is gone,   66
  And there is nothing left remarkable
  Beneath the visiting moon.
      [Swoons.]
CHARMIAN O, quietness, lady!
IRAS She's dead too, our sovereign.
CHARMIAN Lady!
IRAS Madam!
CHARMIAN O madam, madam, madam!

59 *woo't* wilt thou   64 *garland* . . . *war* flower of all soldiers   65 *pole*
North Star (?)   66 *odds* standard of measurement

IRAS Royal Egypt! Empress!

CHARMIAN Peace, peace, Iras!

CLEOPATRA

No more but e'en a woman, and commanded
By such poor passion as the maid that milks
78 And does the meanest chares. It were for me
To throw my sceptre at the injurious gods,
To tell them that this world did equal theirs
Till they had stol'n our jewel. All's but naught.
82 Patience is sottish, and impatience does
Become a dog that's mad: then is it sin
To rush into the secret house of death
Ere death dare come to us? How do you, women?
What, what! good cheer! Why, how now, Charmian?
My noble girls! Ah, women, women, look!
88 Our lamp is spent, it's out! Good sirs, take heart:
We'll bury him; and then, what's brave, what's noble,
Let's do't after the high Roman fashion,
And make death proud to take us. Come away.
This case of that huge spirit now is cold.
Ah, women, women! Come; we have no friend
But resolution, and the briefest end.

            Exeunt, bearing off Antony's body.

*

V, i   *Enter Caesar, Agrippa, Dolabella, Maecenas,*
        [Gallus, Proculeius,] with his Council of War.

CAESAR

Go to him, Dolabella, bid him yield:
2 Being so frustrate, tell him he mocks
The pauses that he makes.

DOLABELLA   Caesar, I shall.   *[Exit.]*

---

78 *chares* chores   82–83 *Patience . . . mad* both patience and sorrow are now
beside the point   88 *sirs* i.e. Cleopatra's women
V, i The camp of Octavius Caesar   2 *frustrate* helpless   2–3 *he mocks . . .*
makes i.e. to delay surrendering is ridiculous

Enter Decretas, with the sword of Antony.

CAESAR
Wherefore is that ? And what art thou that dar'st
Appear thus to us ?

DECRETAS   I am called Decretas.
Mark Antony I served, who best was worthy
Best to be served. Whilst he stood up and spoke,
He was my master, and I wore my life
To spend upon his haters. If thou please
To take me to thee, as I was to him
I'll be to Caesar ; if thou pleasest not,
I yield thee up my life.

CAESAR   What is't thou say'st ?

DECRETAS
I say, O Caesar, Antony is dead.

CAESAR
The breaking of so great a thing should make
A greater crack. The round world
Should have shook lions into civil streets   16
And citizens to their dens. The death of Antony
Is not a single doom, in the name lay
A moiety of the world.   19

DECRETAS   He is dead, Caesar,
Not by a public minister of justice
Nor by a hirèd knife ; but that self hand   21
Which writ his honor in the acts it did
Hath, with the courage which the heart did lend it,
Splitted the heart. This is his sword,
I robbed his wound of it : behold it stained
With his most noble blood.

CAESAR   Look you sad, friends ?
The gods rebuke me, but it is tidings
To wash the eyes of kings.

AGRIPPA   And strange it is

16 *civil* city   19 *moiety* half   21 *self* same

That nature must compel us to lament
30   Our most persisted deeds.
MAECENAS   His taints and honors
31   Waged equal with him.
AGRIPPA   A rarer spirit never
Did steer humanity; but you, gods, will give us
Some faults to make us men. Caesar is touched.
MAECENAS
When such a spacious mirror 's set before him,
He needs must see himself.
CAESAR   O Antony,
36   I have followed thee to this. But we do launch
Diseases in our bodies. I must perforce
Have shown to thee such a declining day
39   Or look on thine: we could not stall together
In the whole world. But yet let me lament
41   With tears as sovereign as the blood of hearts
42   That thou, my brother, my competitor
43   In top of all design, my mate in empire,
Friend and companion in the front of war,
The arm of mine own body, and the heart
46   Where mine his thoughts did kindle – that our stars,
Unreconciliable, should divide
Our equalness to this. Hear me, good friends –
      Enter an Egyptian.
But I will tell you at some meeter season.
50   The business of this man looks out of him;
We'll hear him what he says. Whence are you?
EGYPTIAN
A poor Egyptian yet. The Queen my mistress,
Confined in all she has, her monument,
Of thy intents desires instruction,

---

30 *persisted* i.e. persisted in   31 *Waged equal with* were evenly balanced in
36 *launch* lance   39 *stall* dwell   41 *sovereign* potent   42 *competitor*
partner   43 *In . . . design* in every lofty enterprise   46 *his* its   50 *looks . . .
him* shows in his eyes

That she preparèdly may frame herself
To th' way she's forced to.

CAESAR   Bid her have good heart:
She soon shall know of us, by some of ours,
How honorable and how kindly we
Determine for her. For Caesar cannot live
To be ungentle.

EGYPTIAN   So the gods preserve thee!   *Exit.*

CAESAR
Come hither, Proculeius. Go and say
We purpose her no shame: give her what comforts
The quality of her passion shall require,   63
Lest, in her greatness, by some mortal stroke
She do defeat us. For her life in Rome
Would be eternal in our triumph. Go,   66
And with your speediest bring us what she says
And how you find of her.

PROCULEIUS   Caesar, I shall.   *Exit.*

CAESAR
Gallus, go you along. *[Exit Gallus.]* Where's Dolabella,
To second Proculeius?

ALL   Dolabella!

CAESAR
Let him alone, for I remember now
How he's employed. He shall in time be ready.
Go with me to my tent, where you shall see
How hardly I was drawn into this war,
How calm and gentle I proceeded still
In all my writings. Go with me, and see   76
What I can show in this.   *Exeunt.*

*

63 *passion* grief   66 *eternal* eternally memorable   76 *writings* dispatches
(to Antony)

V, ii   *Enter Cleopatra, Charmian, Iras, and Mardian.*

CLEOPATRA

My desolation does begin to make

2   A better life. 'Tis paltry to be Caesar:

3   Not being Fortune, he's but Fortune's knave,

A minister of her will. And it is great

To do that thing that ends all other deeds,

Which shackles accidents and bolts up change;

7   Which sleeps, and never palates more the dung,

The beggar's nurse and Caesar's.

        Enter [to the gates of the monument] Proculeius.

PROCULEIUS

Caesar sends greeting to the Queen of Egypt,

And bids thee study on what fair demands

Thou mean'st to have him grant thee.

CLEOPATRA   What's thy name?

PROCULEIUS

My name is Proculeius.

CLEOPATRA   Antony

Did tell me of you, bade me trust you, but

14   I do not greatly care to be deceived,

That have no use for trusting. If your master

Would have a queen his beggar, you must tell him

That majesty, to keep decorum, must

No less beg than a kingdom: if he please

To give me conquered Egypt for my son,

20   He gives me so much of mine own as I

Will kneel to him with thanks.

PROCULEIUS   Be of good cheer:

Y' are fall'n into a princely hand, fear nothing.

23   Make your full reference freely to my lord,

Who is so full of grace that it flows over

On all that need. Let me report to him

V, ii *Before the monument of Cleopatra* 2 *A better life* i.e. a truer estimate
of values 3 *knave* servant 7 *dung* i.e. the fruits of earth, which is everybody's nurse 14 *to be deceived* whether I am deceived or not 20 *as* that
23 *Make ... reference* entrust your case

Your sweet dependency, and you shall find
A conqueror that will pray in aid for kindness,   27
Where he for grace is kneeled to.
CLEOPATRA   Pray you, tell him
I am his fortune's vassal, and I send him
The greatness he has got. I hourly learn   30
A doctrine of obedience, and would gladly
Look him i' th' face.
PROCULEIUS   This I'll report, dear lady.
Have comfort, for I know your plight is pitied
Of him that caused it.
          [*Enter Roman Soldiers into the monument.*]
You see how easily she may be surprised.
          [*They seize Cleopatra.*]
Guard her till Caesar come
IRAS Royal Queen!
CHARMIAN O Cleopatra! thou art taken, Queen.
CLEOPATRA
Quick, quick, good hands!
          [*Draws a dagger.*]
PROCULEIUS   Hold, worthy lady, hold!
          [*Disarms her.*]
Do not yourself such wrong, who are in this
Relieved, but not betrayed.   41
CLEOPATRA   What, of death too,
That rids our dogs of languish?   42
PROCULEIUS   Cleopatra,
Do not abuse my master's bounty by
Th' undoing of yourself: let the world see
His nobleness well acted, which your death   45
Will never let come forth.
CLEOPATRA   Where art thou, death?
Come hither, come: come, come, and take a queen
Worth many babes and beggars!

27 *pray . . . kindness* ask your aid in naming kindnesses he can do for you
30 *got* i.e. won from me   41 *Relieved* rescued   42 *languish* pain   45 *acted*
put into effect

PROCULEIUS   O, temperance, lady!
CLEOPATRA
Sir, I will eat no meat, I'll not drink, sir –
50   If idle talk will once be necessary –
I'll not sleep neither. This mortal house I'll ruin,
Do Caesar what he can. Know, sir, that I
Will not wait pinioned at your master's court
Nor once be chastised with the sober eye
Of dull Octavia. Shall they hoist me up
56   And show me to the shouting varletry
Of censuring Rome? Rather a ditch in Egypt
Be gentle grave unto me! Rather on Nilus' mud
Lay me stark-nak'd and let the waterflies
60   Blow me into abhorring! Rather make
My country's high pyramides my gibbet
And hang me up in chains!
PROCULEIUS   You do extend
These thoughts of horror further than you shall
Find cause in Caesar.
           Enter Dolabella.
DOLABELLA   Proculeius,
What thou hast done thy master Caesar knows,
And he hath sent me for thee. For the Queen,
I'll take her to my guard.
PROCULEIUS   So, Dolabella,
It shall content me best: be gentle to her.
           [To Cleopatra]
To Caesar I will speak what you shall please,
If you'll employ me to him.
70 CLEOPATRA   Say, I would die.
                     Exit Proculeius [with Soldiers].

DOLABELLA
Most noble Empress, you have heard of me?
CLEOPATRA
I cannot tell.

---

50 *If . . . necessary* even if I must for the present moment resort to words,
not acts **56** *varletry* mob **60** *Blow me* make me swell

DOLABELLA   Assuredly you know me.
CLEOPATRA
   No matter, sir, what I have heard or known.
   You laugh when boys or women tell their dreams;
   Is't not your trick?
DOLABELLA   I understand not, madam.
CLEOPATRA
   I dreamt there was an Emperor Antony.
   O, such another sleep, that I might see
   But such another man.
DOLABELLA   If it might please ye –
CLEOPATRA
   His face was as the heav'ns, and therein stuck
   A sun and moon, which kept their course and lighted
   The little O, th' earth.   81
DOLABELLA   Most sovereign creature –
CLEOPATRA
   His legs bestrid the ocean: his reared arm
   Crested the world: his voice was propertied   83
   As all the tunèd spheres, and that to friends;
   But when he meant to quail and shake the orb,   85
   He was as rattling thunder. For his bounty,
   There was no winter in't: an autumn 'twas
   That grew the more by reaping: his delights   88
   Were dolphin-like, thy showed his back above
   The element they lived in: in his livery
   Walked crowns and crownets: realms and islands were   91
   As plates dropped from his pocket.   92
DOLABELLA   Cleopatra –
CLEOPATRA
   Think you there was or might be such a man
   As this I dreamt of?

81 *Th'* . . . *earth* (the generally accepted rendering of a folio reading which
may possibly mean something quite different: 'The little o' th' earth')
83–84 *was propertied As* i.e. made music like   85 *quail* cow; *orb* earth
88–90 *his* . . . *lived in* i.e. he rose above the pleasures that he lived in as the
dolphin rises above the surface of the sea   91 *crowns and crownets* i.e.
kings and princes   92 *plates* coins

DOLABELLA   Gentle madam, no.
CLEOPATRA
    You lie, up to the hearing of the gods.
    But if there be nor ever were one such,
97 It's past the size of dreaming : nature wants stuff
    To vie strange forms with fancy, yet t' imagine
    An Antony were nature's piece 'gainst fancy,
    Condemning shadows quite.
DOLABELLA   Hear me, good madam.
    Your loss is as yourself, great ; and you bear it
102 As answering to the weight. Would I might never
    O'ertake pursued success but I do feel,
    By the rebound of yours, a grief that smites
    My very heart at root.
CLEOPATRA   I thank you, sir.
    Know you what Caesar means to do with me ?
DOLABELLA
    I am loath to tell you what I would you knew.
CLEOPATRA
    Nay, pray you, sir.
DOLABELLA   Though he be honorable –
CLEOPATRA
    He'll lead me, then, in triumph ?
DOLABELLA
    Madam, he will. I know't.
            Flourish. Enter Proculeius, Caesar, Gallus,
            Maecenas, [Seleucus,] and others of his Train.
ALL
    Make way there ! Caesar !
CAESAR
    Which is the Queen of Egypt ?

97–100 *nature . . . quite* i.e. nature rarely can compete with man's imagination in creating outstanding forms of excellence, but if she created an
Antony, he would be her masterpiece, outdoing the unreal images of
imagination altogether 102–03 *Would . . . do* i.e. may I never have success
if I do not

DOLABELLA
    It is the Emperor, madam.
        Cleopatra kneels.

CAESAR
    Arise! You shall not kneel:
    I pray you rise, rise, Egypt.

CLEOPATRA   Sir, the gods
    Will have it thus. My master and my lord
    I must obey.

CAESAR   Take to you no hard thoughts.
    The record of what injuries you did us,
    Though written in our flesh, we shall remember
    As things but done by chance.

CLEOPATRA   Sole sir o' th' world,
    I cannot project mine own cause so well   121
    To make it clear, but do confess I have
    Been laden with like frailties which before
    Have often shamed our sex.

CAESAR   Cleopatra, know,
    We will extenuate rather than enforce.   125
    If you apply yourself to our intents,   126
    Which towards you are most gentle, you shall find
    A benefit in this change; but if you seek
    To lay on me a cruelty by taking
    Antony's course, you shall bereave yourself
    Of my good purposes, and put your children
    To that destruction which I'll guard them from
    If thereon you rely. I'll take my leave.

CLEOPATRA
    And may, through all the world: 'tis yours, and we,
    Your scutcheons and your signs of conquest, shall   135
    Hang in what place you please. Here, my good lord.
        [Offering a scroll.]

---

121 *project* set forth   125 *enforce* emphasize (them)   126 *apply* conform
135 *scutcheons* victor's trappings

CAESAR
You shall advise me in all for Cleopatra.

CLEOPATRA
138 This is the brief of money, plate, and jewels
I am possessed of. 'Tis exactly valued,
Not petty things admitted. Where's Seleucus?

SELEUCUS
Here, madam.

CLEOPATRA
This is my treasurer; let him speak, my lord,
Upon his peril, that I have reserved
To myself nothing. Speak the truth, Seleucus.

SELEUCUS
Madam,
146 I had rather seel my lips than to my peril
Speak that which is not.

CLEOPATRA   What have I kept back?

SELEUCUS
Enough to purchase what you have made known.

CAESAR
Nay, blush not, Cleopatra, I approve
Your wisdom in the deed.

CLEOPATRA   See, Caesar: O, behold,
151 How pomp is followed! Mine will now be yours,
152 And should we shift estates, yours would be mine.
The ingratitude of this Seleucus does
Even make me wild. O slave, of no more trust
Than love that's hired! What, goest thou back? Thou
    shalt
Go back, I warrant thee; but I'll catch thine eyes,
Though they had wings. Slave, soulless villain, dog!
O rarely base!

CAESAR   Good Queen, let us entreat you.

CLEOPATRA
O Caesar, what a wounding shame is this,

138 *brief* résumé 146 *seel* sew up 151 *Mine* i.e. my followers 152 *estates* positions

That thou vouchsafing here to visit me,
Doing the honor of thy lordliness
To one so meek, that mine own servant should
Parcel the sum of my disgraces by   163
Addition of his envy. Say, good Caesar,
That I some lady trifles have reserved,   165
Immoment toys, things of such dignity   166
As we greet modern friends withal; and say   167
Some nobler token I have kept apart
For Livia and Octavia, to induce
Their mediation – must I be unfolded
With one that I have bred? The gods! It smites me   171
Beneath the fall I have. [to Seleucus] Prithee go hence,
Or I shall show the cinders of my spirits   173
Through th' ashes of my chance. Wert thou a man,   174
Thou wouldst have mercy on me.

CAESAR   Forbear, Seleucus.
                               [Exit Seleucus.]

CLEOPATRA
Be it known that we, the greatest, are misthought   176
For things that others do; and, when we fall,
We answer others' merits in our name,   178
Are therefore to be pitied.

CAESAR   Cleopatra,
Not what you have reserved, nor what acknowledged,
Put we i' th' roll of conquest: still be't yours,
Bestow it at your pleasure, and believe   182
Caesar's no merchant, to make prize with you   183
Of things that merchants sold. Therefore be cheered,
Make not your thoughts your prisons: no, dear Queen,   185
For we intend so to dispose you as   186
Yourself shall give us counsel. Feed and sleep:

163 *Parcel* piece out further 165 *lady* feminine 166 *Immoment* of no
moment 167 *modern* common 171 *With* by 173 *cinders* burning coals
174 *chance* fortune 176 *misthought* misjudged 178 *merits . . . name*
misdeeds done in our name (as if Seleucus had falsified the inventory for
his own gain) 182 *Bestow* use 183 *make prize* haggle 185 *Make . . .
prisons* i.e. only in your own conception are you a prisoner 186 *you* of you

Our care and pity is so much upon you
That we remain your friend; and so adieu.

CLEOPATRA
My master, and my lord!

CAESAR   Not so. Adieu.
                    Flourish. Exeunt Caesar, and his Train.

CLEOPATRA
191   He words me, girls, he words me, that I should not
192   Be noble to myself! But hark thee, Charmian.
                    [Whispers Charmian.]

IRAS
Finish, good lady, the bright day is done,
And we are for the dark.

CLEOPATRA   Hie thee again:
I have spoke already, and it is provided;
Go put it to the haste.

CHARMIAN   Madam, I will.
                    Enter Dolabella.

DOLABELLA
Where's the Queen?

CHARMIAN   Behold, sir.   *[Exit.]*

CLEOPATRA   Dolabella!

DOLABELLA
Madam, as thereto sworn, by your command
(Which my love makes religion to obey)
200   I tell you this: Caesar through Syria
Intends his journey, and within three days
You with your children will he send before.
Make your best use of this. I have performed
Your pleasure, and my promise.

CLEOPATRA   Dolabella,
I shall remain your debtor.

DOLABELLA   I your servant.
Adieu, good Queen; I must attend on Caesar.

191 *words* deceives with words   192 *noble* i.e. by suicide

CLEOPATRA
Farewell, and thanks.   *Exit [Dolabella]*.
                    Now, Iras, what think'st thou?
Thou, an Egyptian puppet, shall be shown
In Rome as well as I: mechanic slaves
With greasy aprons, rules, and hammers shall
Uplift us to the view. In their thick breaths,
Rank of gross diet, shall we be enclouded,   212
And forced to drink their vapor.
IRAS   The gods forbid!
CLEOPATRA
Nay, 'tis most certain, Iras. Saucy lictors   214
Will catch at us like strumpets, and scald rhymers   215
Ballad us out o' tune. The quick comedians
Extemporally will stage us, and present
Our Alexandrian revels: Antony
Shall be brought drunken forth, and I shall see
Some squeaking Cleopatra boy my greatness   220
I' th' posture of a whore.
IRAS   O the good gods!
CLEOPATRA
Nay, that's certain.
IRAS
I'll never see't! for I am sure my nails
Are stronger than mine eyes.
CLEOPATRA   Why, that's the way
To fool their preparation, and to conquer
Their most absurd intents.
        Enter Charmian.   Now, Charmian!
Show me, my women, like a queen: go fetch
My best attires. I am again for Cydnus,
To meet Mark Antony. Sirrah Iras, go.
Now, noble Charmian, we'll dispatch indeed,
And when thou hast done this chare, I'll give thee leave   231

212 *Rank of* offensive because of   214 *lictors* officers   215 *scald* scabby
220 *squeaking* i.e. because women's parts were acted by young boys; *boy*
satirize   231 *chare* chore

To play till doomsday. – Bring our crown and all.
                    [Exit Iras.] A noise within.
  Wherefore's this noise?
    Enter a Guardsman.

GUARDSMAN   Here is a rural fellow
  That will not be denied your Highness' presence:
  He brings you figs.

CLEOPATRA
  Let him come in.   *Exit Guardsman.*
                    What poor an instrument
  May do a noble deed! He brings me liberty.
238   My resolution's placed, and I have nothing
  Of woman in me: now from head to foot
  I am marble-constant: now the fleeting moon
241   No planet is of mine.
      Enter Guardsman and Clown [with basket].
GUARDSMAN   This is the man.

CLEOPATRA
242   Avoid, and leave him.   *Exit Guardsman.*
243   Hast thou the pretty worm of Nilus there,
  That kills and pains not?

CLOWN Truly I have him; but I would not be the party
  that should desire you to touch him, for his biting is
247   immortal: those that do die of it do seldom or never
  recover.

CLEOPATRA Remember'st thou any that have died on't?

CLOWN Very many, men and women too. I heard of one
251   of them no longer than yesterday; a very honest woman,
  but something given to lie, as a woman should not do
  but in the way of honesty – how she died of the biting
  of it, what pain she felt. Truly, she makes a very good
  report o' th' worm; but he that will believe all that they
  say shall never be saved by half that they do; but this is

238 *placed* fixed   241 s.d. *Clown* rustic   242 *Avoid* go   243 *worm* serpent
(asp)   247 *immortal* mortal, i.e. deadly (the rustic blunders in speech here
and below)   251 *honest* respectable

most falliable, the worm's an odd worm.   257

CLEOPATRA Get thee hence, farewell.

CLOWN I wish you all joy of the worm.
  [Sets down his basket.]

CLEOPATRA Farewell.

CLOWN You must think this, look you, that the worm
 will do his kind.   262

CLEOPATRA Ay, ay; farewell.

CLOWN Look you, the worm is not to be trusted but in the
 keeping of wise people: for indeed there is no goodness
 in the worm.

CLEOPATRA Take thou no care, it shall be heeded.

CLOWN Very good. Give it nothing, I pray you, for it is
 not worth the feeding.

CLEOPATRA Will it eat me?

CLOWN You must not think I am so simple but I know the
 devil himself will not eat a woman: I know that a
 woman is a dish for the gods, if the devil dress her not.   273
 But truly, these same whoreson devils do the gods great
 harm in their women; for in every ten that they make,
 the devils mar five.

CLEOPATRA Well, get thee gone, farewell.

CLOWN Yes, forsooth. I wish you joy o' th' worm.   *Exit.*
 [Enter Iras with a robe, crown, etc.]

CLEOPATRA
Give me my robe, put on my crown, I have
Immortal longings in me. Now no more
The juice of Egypt's grape shall moist this lip.
Yare, yare, good Iras; quick. Methinks I hear   282
Antony call: I see him rouse himself
To praise my noble act. I hear him mock
The luck of Caesar, which the gods give men
To excuse their after wrath. Husband, I come:

---

257 *falliable* (an error for 'infallible')   262 *his kind* i.e. what may be expected
from his species   273 *dress* (with pun on the culinary sense)   282 *Yare*
nimbly

Now to that name my courage prove my title!
288   I am fire, and air; my other elements
       I give to baser life. So, have you done?
       Come then, and take the last warmth of my lips.
       Farewell, kind Charmian, Iras, long farewell.
              [Kisses them. Iras falls and dies.] *took poison*
292   Have I the aspic in my lips? Dost fall?
       If thou and nature can so gently part,
       The stroke of death is as a lover's pinch,
       Which hurts, and is desired. Dost thou lie still?
       If thus thou vanishest, thou tell'st the world
       It is not worth leave-taking.

CHARMIAN
       Dissolve, thick cloud, and rain, that I may say
       The gods themselves do weep.

CLEOPATRA   This proves me base:
       If she first meet the curlèd Antony,
       He'll make demand of her, and spend that kiss
       Which is my heaven to have. Come, thou mortal wretch,
              [To an asp, which she applies to her breast.]
303   With thy sharp teeth this knot intrinsicate
       Of life at once untie. Poor venomous fool,
305   Be angry, and dispatch. O, couldst thou speak,
       That I might hear thee call great Caesar ass
307   Unpolicied!

CHARMIAN   O Eastern star!

CLEOPATRA   Peace, peace!
       Dost thou not see my baby at my breast,
       That sucks the nurse asleep?

CHARMIAN   O, break! O, break!

CLEOPATRA
       As sweet as balm, as soft as air, as gentle –

---

288 *fire, and air* (the lighter of the four elements, thought of as belonging
to immortality); *other elements* i.e. water and earth, the heavier elements,
bequeathed by Cleopatra to mortality **292** *aspic* asp **303** *intrinsicate*
intricate **305** *dispatch* make haste **307** *Unpolicied* outwitted

O Antony ! Nay, I will take thee too :
    [Applies another asp to her arm.]
What should I stay –
        Dies.

CHARMIAN
    In this wild world ? So, fare thee well.
    Now boast thee, death, in thy possession lies
    A lass unparalleled. Downy windows, close ;   *Shuts eyes*
    And golden Phoebus never be beheld
    Of eyes again so royal ! Your crown 's awry ;
    I'll mend it, and then play –
        Enter the Guard, rustling in.

1 . GUARDSMAN
    Where's the Queen ?
CHARMIAN   Speak softly, wake her not.
1 . GUARDSMAN
    Caesar hath sent –
CHARMIAN   Too slow a messenger.
        [Applies an asp.]
    O, come apace, dispatch, I partly feel thee.
1 . GUARDSMAN
    Approach, ho ! All's not well : Caesar 's beguiled.   322
2 . GUARDSMAN
    There's Dolabella sent from Caesar. Call him.
1 . GUARDSMAN
    What work is here ! Charmian, is this well done ?
CHARMIAN
    It is well done, and fitting for a princess
    Descended of so many royal kings.
    Ah, soldier !
        Charmian dies.
        Enter Dolabella.
DOLABELLA
    How goes it here ?
2 . GUARDSMAN   All dead.

322 *beguiled* tricked

DOLABELLA   Caesar, thy thoughts
329   Touch their effects in this : thyself art coming
To see performed the dreaded act which thou
So sought'st to hinder.
Enter Caesar and all his Train, marching.
ALL   A way there, a way for Caesar !
DOLABELLA
O sir, you are too sure an augurer :
That you did fear is done.
CAESAR   Bravest at the last,
334   She levelled at our purposes, and being royal,
Took her own way. The manner of their deaths ?
I do not see them bleed.
DOLABELLA   Who was last with them ?
I. GUARDSMAN
A simple countryman, that brought her figs.
This was his basket.
CAESAR   Poisoned, then.
I. GUARDSMAN   O Caesar,
This Charmian lived but now, she stood and spake ;
I found her trimming up the diadem
On her dead mistress ; tremblingly she stood,
And on the sudden dropped.
CAESAR   O noble weakness !
If they had swallowed poison, 'twould appear
By external swelling ; but she looks like sleep,
As she would catch another Antony
346   In her strong toil of grace.
DOLABELLA   Here on her breast
347   There is a vent of blood, and something blown ;
The like is on her arm.
I. GUARDSMAN
This is an aspic's trail, and these fig leaves
Have slime upon them, such as th' aspic leaves
Upon the caves of Nile.

329 *Touch their effects* meet fulfillment   334 *levelled at* guessed   346 *toil*
net   347 *vent* discharge; *blown* swelled

CAESAR   Most probable
That so she died : for her physician tells me
She hath pursued conclusions infinite   353
Of easy ways to die. Take up her bed,
And bear her women from the monument.
She shall be buried by her Antony.
No grave upon the earth shall clip in it   357
A pair so famous. High events as these
Strike those that make them ; and their story is   359
No less in pity than his glory which
Brought them to be lamented. Our army shall
In solemn show attend this funeral,
And then to Rome. Come, Dolabella, see
High order in this great solemnity.   *Exeunt omnes.*

353 *conclusions* experiments   357 *clip* clasp   359 *Strike* touch